No Trespassing

Rachelle Jarred

No Trespassing Copyright and Disclaimer

The information and images contained in this book, including cover art, are protected under all Federal and International Copyright Laws and Treaties. Therefore, any use or reprint of the material in the book, either paperback or electronic, is prohibited. Users may not transmit or reproduce the material in any way shape or form – mechanically or electronically such as recording, photocopying, or information storage and retrieval system – without getting prior written permission from the publisher/author.

All attempts have been made to verify the information contained in this book, _No Trespassing_, but the author and publisher do not bear any responsibility for errors or omissions. Any perceived negative connotation of any individual, group, or company is purely unintentional. Furthermore, this book is intended as entertainment only and as such, any and all responsibility for actions taken in reading this book lies with the reader alone and not with the author or publisher. This book is not intended as medical, legal, or business advice and the reader alone holds sole responsibility for any consequences of any actions taken after reading this book. Additionally, it is the reader's responsibility alone and not the author's or publisher's to ensure that all applicable laws and regulations for the business practice are adhered to.

Copyright © 2018 BluGem Publishing, LLC

DEDICATION

A Word From The Author

I would like to thank God for blessing me with the gift of writing. I would also like to thank my significant other for being here, and for supporting my dreams. I also dedicate this book to my children; thank you for making me proud to be your mother. To my mother for being there, my dad who is looking down on me from heaven, my friends, and my family: I thank you all for your continuous love and support.

To my readers:

I would like to thank you all for continuing to read my novels and following me on my journey. Also, thank you for making my first novel, <u>Nymphopervtress: The Desiree Logan Story #3,</u> known and loved enough to be featured on Amazon's Top Best-Selling List.

Contents

Chapter One:

The Weekend Begins

B *rrring!*

"I'm so glad it's Friday. We couldn't have gotten out of there fast enough," Parker said as he adjusted his backpack and they made their way off school property.

"You can say that again," Melody said. Sammy and Patty were walking behind them, talking about the scores they received on their math test. Parker kept sneaking glances at Melody as they walked side by side. He admired the way she wore her hair and the way she dressed. He had the biggest crush on her, but he didn't think she would ever like him. Why would she? He was scared of everything and got bullied on a daily basis. Not only at school, but by his big brother, Marvin, as well. One of these days, he was going to prove himself to her.

As the four friends were making their way down the street, they stopped in front of the abandoned Grady Hospital.

"This place is creepy," Parker said.

"It's not all that bad, Parker," his best friend, Sammy, said. "It just looks creepy on the outside."

"And it's probably covered with filth and spiderwebs on the inside," Melody said, shivering.

"Hey, check it out," Patty said, motioning them over to a sign on the gate. "Hey, Parker, isn't Forman and Smith your dad's construction company?"

"Yeah, so?" Parker said stepping closer.

"It says they're knocking this place down this Sunday."

"Good riddance," Parker replied.

"Exactly," Melody said in agreement. "This horrific looking place should have been torn down years ago, if you ask me."

"But nobody asked you," Sammy said, butting in. "We should go inside, just to see what it's like."

"Let's do it," Patty said, standing beside him and getting ready to go in. Parker jumped in front of them to stop them.

"I don't think that's a good idea, you guys," Parker replied.

"Why not?" Patty asked.

"You guys don't know what's in there," he responded.

"Even more reason why we should go," Sammy said, pushing Parker aside. Patty and Sammy made their way to the steps and looked back.

"What are you two waiting for?" Sammy asked Melody and Parker.

"I'm not doing this with you and Patty," Parker said.

"Neither am I," Melody replied. "You guys are crazy."

She and Parker continued walking. They walked a few feet and turned around to see Sammy and Patty jogging towards them.

"You guys are chickens," Patty said lightly pinching Melody's arm. "And Parker, you're the biggest chicken of all."

"Leave him alone, Patty," Melody said, taking up for Parker. She placed a hand on his shoulder and he beamed inside.

"Puk, puk, pukaaak," Patty said, imitating a chicken as she made pecking motions at both Melody and Parker. Sammy burst out in laughter.

"Okay, okay, Patty. Enough," Sammy said, throwing an arm around Parker's shoulder. "If he's scared, let him be scared."

"But I'm not scared," Parker said turning red.

"If you say so," Patty replied. The twelve-year-olds continued on home. Halfway down the street, they saw a homeless man.

"Hey guys, there's Petey," Melody said.

"What do you guys have left over from lunch?"

The friends all opened their backpacks and pulled out their food as they walked closer to Petey. When he saw the kids, he sat up and smiled.

No Trespassing

"Hi, kids," he said to them in a raspy, dry voice. His voice was practically leaving him from sleeping on the cold ground all hours of the day and night.

"Here's some food for you, Petey," Patty said as she handed him the other half of a ham sandwich. With gratitude, he took it and smiled. Parker handed him a bag of chips and a Capri Sun juice pouch. Sammy handed him a Ziploc bag of grapes, and Melody gave him the extra muffin she had packed just for him.

"Do you guys have any change for him?" Patty asked. They all dug into their pockets and dropped what all they had into Petey's cup. They told him they would see him after school on Monday and they waved goodbye to him. He smiled back showing a big hole where teeth once lived. They made it to the street corner and went their separate ways.

✶✶✶✶

"I don't understand what you could possibly see in Parker," Patty said to Melody as they crossed the street.

"I don't know either," Melody responded with a shrug of her shoulders. "He's cute, and he's really sweet."

"Yeah, yeah, yeah. If you say so, Mel. All I'm saying is that Parker needs to get some heart. If he doesn't, people are gonna always push him around."

"You mean people like you?" she said, stopping in her tracks.

"Yeah, people like me," Patty replied in defense. "I love Parker like a brother. I only pick on him to toughen him up."

"Maybe you can talk to him like a normal person, Pat. Nobody deserves to get bullied. Especially by people that are supposed to be his friends." Melody continued to walk as Patty stopped in her tracks.

I do pick on him a lot, she thought to herself. *Maybe I was wrong in her eyes. In mine, I was just doing my part as a friend. Forget what Melody says. Parker needs to grow a backbone and stop letting people push him around. That's his problem, not mine. All I can do is be a friend and hope that, one of these days, he would be brave enough to stick up for himself.* She quickly jogged up to where Melody was; she was walking onto her front porch.

"Hey, I'm gonna just call you later, okay?" Melody said to me as she inserted the key into the lock.

"Are you seriously mad at me, Mel? Come on now," Patty replied.

"I'm not mad about anything. I'm just tired, that's all. Besides, I have a lot of homework to do."

"Oh, okay. Well, I guess I'll talk to you later," Patty said reaching out for a hug. Reluctantly, Melody hugged her back.

✳✳✳✳

"I'm sorry about what I said back there, bro., Sammy said to Parker. They crossed Mason Street and continued to walk to their houses.

"It's okay, Sam. I'm just so sick and tired of everybody calling me a chicken and a scaredy cat."

"So, what are you gonna do about it?"

"I don't know," Parker said, shrugging his shoulders. "Why does everybody have to pick on the quiet kid? I haven't done anything to anybody."

"That doesn't matter, Parker. I thought you would know that by now. Kids are cruel and now that I think about it, so am I. I'm supposed to be your best friend and I do you the same way."

"That's just because you be having fun," Parker said with a slight laugh. Sammy stopped him.

"That still doesn't make it right. Having fun shouldn't involve hurting my best friend's feelings, and I'm sorry," Sammy said, reaching his hand out. Parker took it and shook his hand.

"Now that we got that out of the way, want to come over and play Fortnite?"

"I can't tonight, but maybe tomorrow, after practice. I have a report due Monday on the Civil War for history class."

"Yikes," Parker replied. "You have fun with that, buddy."

"Yeah, right," Sammy said, laughing. They reached the corner of Sutton and Cobblestone and went to their separate residences. They waved at one another from their porches before entering their houses.

****

"I'm really sorry about today, Parker," Melody said into the phone. She had called to apologize on behalf of their obnoxious friends.

"It's cool, Mel. They were just trying to have fun and scare us."

"Trying to? I was scared. Nothing about that creepy hospital spells fun for me."

"Yeah, I know what you mean. But, honestly, do you ever think about what could possibly be left in that place?"

"No, and I don't want to," Melody shrieked.

"I wonder what happened. Why would they close down the closest hospital in town? Now we have to go almost an hour away to get to an emergency room. That's crazy."

"I don't care, Parker," Melody snapped. "Look, I apologize for my outburst but seriously, stop it. Your dad is knocking that building down and I'm sure there is a good reason behind it. Stop pressing the issue. It's not that important."

"You're right."

Knock. Knock.

Parker's door opened and his mother popped her head inside. "Sweetheart, dinner will be ready in ten."

"Okay," he replied. She closed the door and headed down the hallway. "Look, Mel, I have to go. I will see you tomorrow.'

"Talk to you later, Parker," she said, hanging up.

Parker placed his cordless phone on the charger. He sat and thought about the abandoned hospital. He wondered what secrets could possibly lie within those molded walls. He went over to his computer and opened the Internet Explorer page. As soon as typed in Grady HospitaL and hit the enter key, his older brother, Marvin, walked into his room.

"Mom, told me to come and get you, weasel."

"Don't you know how to knock, jerk?"

"Yeah, I do, but since it's you, I bother not to. Unless you want to do something about it," Marvin said, folding his arms and leaning against the wall.

"You get on my nerves, Marvin. I wish you would hurry up and get out of the house already."

"Keep dreaming, squirt," he replied before walking over to where Parker was. He gave him a wedgie and pushed him onto the bed. He ran out the room and ran downstairs.

That dude really grinds my gears, Parker thought. *One of these days, I was going to stand up to him and sock him one good time. He will probably kick my butt really bad, but at least I would stand up to him. That's all that matters, right?* He put his computer in sleep mode and went to the bathroom. He washed his hands and dried them on the towel. Before he left the bathroom, he looked at himself in the mirror. *Nobody would be scared of me. I wouldn't even be scared of me. I'm frail, and lacked muscles. I was puny to say the least. No wonder I was so afraid of everything and everyone; they were all bigger than me.*

✳✳✳✳

"So, guys, how was school today?" Parker's mom, Elaine, asked her two sons across the dinner table.

"It was freaking awesome, Mom," his brother, Marvin, replied. "I aced my math test and got a chance to catch the girls' volleyball team at practice."

"Really, Marvin?" their mother responded.

"Oh yeah, sorry," he said, still smiling. The table had gotten silent. Their father, Eliot, noticed that Parker wasn't eating and seemed a little distracted. He broke the silence and asked him what was wrong.

"Is it true that you're going to knock down the old Grady Hospital?" he asked as he toyed with his vegetables.

"Yeah, son. Why, is that bothering you?"

"It's not, really. I was just wondering. My friends and I saw the sign on the gate when we passed by it after school today."

"Oh, okay. But, Parker, that building has been needing to come down. And I'm glad that the time has come to do so," Eliot replied.

"You know, legend has it that there was this guy named Willie McNair that haunted that old place," Marvin said.

"Who's Willie McNair?" Parker asked as his eyes grew with fear.

No Trespassing

"He was a patient there back in 1973 that had gone ballistic and killed everyone in the hospital. Unfortunately, he had never been caught," Marvin responded.

"Knock it off, Marvin," Parker replied. "You're just trying to scare me."

"Uh-uh, no I'm not. And you know what else I heard?"

"What?" Parker asked, trembling.

"He loves to kill and eat children," Marvin replied with a sly grin.

"You're lying. Leave me alone, Marvin."

"I'm not lying, little brother. If you think it's a lie, then go see for yourself. Unless you're a chicken," he said, breaking out in laughter.

"I'm not a chicken. Leave me alone, Marvin," Parker yelled at him. but the laughter continued.

"Now, that's enough," their father bellowed.

"Yeah, Marvin. You know your brother is frightened by every little thing," their mother replied with a light snicker.

"I'm not afraid of anything, Mom," he said to her.

"It's okay to be scared, honey," she said, patting his hand.

"I'm not a chicken!" He exclaimed as he snatched his hand away and ran from the dinner table. He ran up to his room and slammed the door. He threw himself onto the bed and buried his face in the pillow. He quickly got back up and grabbed his cell phone. He sent out a group text to his friends, telling them to get flashlights and meet him at the abandoned hospital at 9 o'clock tonight. Just as he put his phone down, Marvin entered his room.

"What are you in here doing, you big chicken? Are you laying eggs for breakfast?" he laughed.

"Shut up and get out of my room," Parker said as he shuffled through his closet looking for a flashlight. He found one and threw it in his backpack.

"Make me," Marvin shot back. Parker glared at him angrily then continued his task. "Where are you going anyways?"

"I'm going to the old Grady Hospital to prove to you, Mom, Dad, and everybody else that I'm not scared of anything."

Marvin burst out into uncontrollable laughter.

"What's so funny, Marvin?

"You're funny. There's no way you're going do it. You're going to chicken out at the last minute. Say you do go inside, Willie McNair will be waiting for you indefinitely."

"That's just a story, and I bet you made it up, just like you do with everything else to scare me."

"If you say so. Just in case you don't make it out alive, can I have your computer?" he asked, grinning from ear to ear.

"Get out of my way," Parker said, quickly brushing past his brother. He ran down the stairs and yelled to his parents that he was going to Sammy's house for the night. They told him that it was okay, and for him to text them as soon as he got there. He promised he would and left the house. He checked his watch and it was a couple of minutes after nine. He hopped on his bike and rode toward the abandoned hospital. Ten minutes had gone by, and he had just joined his friends at the hospital.

"Hey, what gives?" Sammy asked.

"Yeah, Parker?" the girls said in unison.

"I'm ready to go in here. I'm getting tired of everybody calling me a chicken and a scaredy cat."

"But you don't have to go in here to prove that," Melody replied.

He looked at her with sympathetic eyes. "I know that, but I think this is a perfect way. We'll leave at sunrise."

"You cannot be serious right now, Parker," Melody said.

"I'm being as serious as a heart attack right now. Marvin said this place was shut down because of some lunatic. He said that the guy eats and kills people, even children. We're gonna go in here and stay the entire night. Besides, I'm curious to see if there are any dead bodies left."

Pfft. "I doubt that. If people were killed or something in there, then I would hope there weren't bodies left," Melody replied.

"I'm hypothetically speaking."

No Trespassing

"Hypothetically speaking, if there are any bodies, they are definitely decayed and rotten. Probably smells awful in there. But, we will never know," Melody added.

"You're right about that. We will never know, because we're afraid to go inside," Parker said.

"Not the fact that I'm afraid, but there is also a big sign that says no trespassing. I am *not* breaking the law to do something I may regret later on in my life. That is, if I live to make it."

"So, you're not coming?" Sammy asked Melody.

"Nope. I'm not going in there, Sam," she said, crossing her arms like a stubborn brat.

"Well, let's go then," Patty said, as she was the first one to hop off her bike. They all leaned their bikes up against the gate before making their way through. Patty stood there as everyone else walked through the gates. She felt an eerie feeling wash over her body and ran to catch up with her friends.

"Okay, I'm coming, too," she said, grabbing Patty's arm. "No way am I staying out here alone." They were getting ready to head up the steps, but Parker stopped them.

"Wait, you guys," Parker said, pulling out his cell phone. "We gotta send the text to our parents that we made it to each other's houses." They all followed in tow as they sent out their messages. Melody was the only one that didn't, because she told her parents that Patty was coming over anyway. They turned back towards the creepy hospital.

"Everybody ready?" Sammy asked.

They all looked back and forth at one another before they all replied, "Yep."

Parker led the way and Patty and Melody held onto one another as Sammy followed closely behind. They forced the rickety hospital door open and closed it back so no one would notice that somebody had gone inside.

"See, this isn't so bad," Sammy said as he waved the flashlight around at different parts of the room. Melody freaked out when she saw how close she was to touching a spider web. She shrieked and became upset, because she could have easily ruined her new cashmere sweater.

"Let's go, guys," Parker said, waving his hand to his friends. They walked closer together as they walked further into the hospital.

"Ahhhh," they all yelled at the top of their lungs when they heard the door of the room they had just entered through slam.

"We need to go back," Parker said, breathing heavily.

"We're not going anywhere, Parker," Sammy interjected. "You said you wanted to face your fears and stay until sunrise. And as for that, we have eight hours before that happens."

"What about our parents, Sammy?" Melody cried.

"Chill out, Melody. They're probably asleep by now. Besides, they probably think you're in your room hanging with Patty anyway. Remember? So, come on," he said, starting to walk again. Melody, Patty, and Parker exchanged worried looks at one another. They all knew that they should just leave, but Sammy didn't want to. And what kind of friends would they be if they just left him?

As they walked further down the halls, the lights suddenly flickered on. "Who did that?" Parker asked, stammering over his words. They all clicked their flashlights off.

"I don't know," the girls said in unison.

"I thought this place was supposed to be abandoned, Parker?"

"It is," he replied.

"Then how does it have power?" she asked in a panic.

"Will you all just calm down? *Sheesh*. It might have just been the generator," Sammy replied.

"A generator in an abandoned building? Really, Sammy? Does that make any sense to you at all?" Melody exclaimed.

"No, it doesn't, Melody, but what else could it be? Do you have a better explanation than mine?" he asked, staring at her. Melody just stared back with angry eyes and remained silent. She stormed off a few feet down the hall. Patty went down the hall after her to try and calm her down.

"Hey, guys wait up," Parker yelled behind them. "We have to go after them, Sammy."

"Man, they will be fine. They're just being girls. They're being scared for no reason whatsoever."

"If you say so."

They walked past old and molded gurneys with dried up blood stains. It seemed as if the further they walked, the stronger the stench was. They covered their noses but that didn't solve anything; the smell continued to burn their eyes. They walked into another one of the hospital rooms. There were medical charts thrown around the room, old clothes, old heart monitors. The place was in complete shambles.

"Hey check this out," Sammy said ,picking up one of the files from the floor. They both looked it over and was shocked. "Isn't Willie McNair the one that allegedly went crazy and killed everyone here? Isn't that what Marvin told you?"

"Yeah," Parker said, swallowing the big lump that had formed in his throat. "And he was never found. Rumor has it that he still wanders these halls, killing trespassers that want to come here and play around."

"We're not trespassers, Parker," Sammy said laughing a little.

"Then what are we? Because we're not supposed to be here."

They heard a loud scream echoing through the halls. They both ran out of the hospital room and listened to see which direction it had come from. They heard the screams again. This time is was two different ones. Melody and Patty were in trouble. They heard footsteps coming towards them. Patty and Melody ran up to them.

"What happened?" Parker asked Melody.

"Somebody grabbed Patty's shoulder back there," she said, crying hysterically, trying to catch her breath.

"Somebody? What are you talking about? There is nobody here but us," Sammy said in defense.

"No, it's not. I saw him with my own eyes. He looked like somebody from the Walking Dead. He was big and had burns on his hands and arms. We need to get out of here before he gets back."

"We are not leaving, Melody. You guys play too much," Sammy replied.

"What are you talking about?" Parker asked. "She said she saw somebody here. What if it's Willie McNair?"

"Oh, please, Parker. You're just afraid to stay here all night, that's all," Sammy replied, leaning up against one of the walls. "Remember, it was your idea to stay all night. So why leave now?"

"That's because I didn't think anybody was here, Sammy," Parker replied. "The girls wouldn't play about anything like this."

"Right," Patty said in agreement.

The room fell silent. They heard light footsteps and groaning coming towards them. They heard a loud thud, and the four kids went running out of the hospital. They all hopped on their bikes and never looked back as they sped down the street. They were riding so fast that they had all separated.

Parker reached his house and hopped off his bike as soon as he pulled up to the gate. He tiptoed on the grass and leaned his bike on the side of the house between the trash cans. At least if his parents headed out before he did, they wouldn't know that he was home already. He walked to the front of the house and looked up to his parents' room. He saw that the tv was still on due to the light on the wall. *Why are they still awake?* he thought as he looked at his phone. It was almost midnight. His parents never stayed up that late. Instead of using the front door, he decided to climb up to his room. He didn't want Marvin to snitch on him either.

He made it to his room and walked as quietly as possible. He put his phone on silent and texted everybody to make sure they were home. Within fifteen minutes, everyone sent a text back.

No Trespassing

Everyone but Sammy.

He called Sammy's phone and didn't get an answer. He waited a few minutes before trying again: still no answer. He had an idea. He peered out of his other bedroom window that faced the street. He looked across the street towards Sammy's house. There were no lights of any sort lit in his house. No tv lights. No bedroom lights. Not thinking much of it, he just figured Sammy had fallen asleep as soon as he got in the house. He took off his clothes and laid down. He had to ease his mind and heart rate. He thought happy thoughts to help him fall into a deep slumber.

Around the corner, Patty and Melody had already made it into Melody's house unnoticed. They were sitting on the floor and taking turns looking out the window as if someone had really been chasing them.

"That was scary," Melody said, finally getting up from the floor after they saw that the coast was clear. She grabbed her pajamas and went into her bathroom.

"Yeah, that was pretty scary," Patty agreed as she swapped her street clothes for pajama pants and a t-shirt. "Did you see how scared Parker was?"

"That wasn't funny, Patty," Melody said, rolling her eyes at Patty as she hopped on her bed. "Did you notice that Sammy didn't text anything in the group chat?" she said as she scrolled through her message threads.

Patty grabbed her phone and did the same. "Yeah, I did notice that. He's probably playing the game or something. You know how Sammy is. He answers messages late all the time, especially on the weekend. Or, maybe he's asleep. They do have baseball practice in the morning."

"That is true," Melody replied as she plugged her phone up to its charger. "Wanna watch some tv before we go to bed?"

"You bet," Patty said, grabbing the remote control and hopping onto Melody's bed as well. "Let's watch the horror movie marathon that they have on AMC."

She flipped through the channels until she came to the correct one. They sat and glued their eyes to the television screen as _Saw 7_ caught their attention.

"I really like this movie," Patty replied as she grabbed a pillow from Melody. "It makes me laugh sometimes. Whoever thought of this movie is a freaking maniac," she said laughing.

"You are one sick individual, Pat. The _Saw_ movies are good, don't get me wrong, but they gross me out. They're not even that scary, honestly."

"I know, but it's better than nothing. It's not boring, so it keeps ahold of my attention."

"Just don't go and get any ideas and try any of this stuff."

"I'm not making any promises," Patty said, laughing maniacally. Melody just stared at her. For the first time in her life, she was actually scared of something. And it just had to be her best friend and her twisted mind. Melody knew that Patty was just kidding, but, then again, sometimes she wasn't too sure. She thought about it again. _Nah. Patty wouldn't hurt me. I have never even seen her hurt a fly. I had nothing to worry about whatsoever._

Back at the abandoned hospital, Sammy was screaming for help. His throat had become dry from the countless hours of screaming. He was scared out of his wits right now. He had made it out of the hospital earlier, right behind his friends, but he didn't make it away. He was running so fast, and wasn't paying attention, he tripped over the broken concrete stairs and sprained both his ankle and his arm. Before he could even grab the attention of his counterparts, they had all rode away on their bikes in fear. Whatever it was that was inside the hospital, had appeared outside and picked him up. Sammy had fought to get free, but the figure was not letting up. He took him back into the abandoned hospital, and out of the possible bystanders' hearing range.

Sammy's heart was racing a mile a minute. He had broken out into a sweat and was panicking. He thought about running away as the hermit looking guy stepped away for a while, but he knew he wasn't gonna make it out. Even if he did, there was no way he was gonna be able to ride his bike to safety. He adjusted his eyes as best as he could in the darkness. At the end of the hall, there was a little dim lighting. The creepy guy was down in one of the rooms. He could see his shadow on the walls.

He dug around into his pockets, feeling for his cell phone. He found it down in the side pocket and pulled it out. He saw that he had missed calls. He went to dial Parker's number back. Breathing heavily again, he listened closely as the phone rang. As soon as Parker picked up the phone with a sleepy, 'Hello,' the call dropped.

Sammy's phone had died.

At that moment, his heart skipped a couple of beats. That was his only hope. How was he gonna escape now? He looked down the hall again and listened. The guy was banging and grunting. Sammy could hear tears of what was probably human flesh or something. Thinking he was gonna be next, he decided to crawl out.

He used his arms to pull himself across the dusty floor, over old and rusty hospital tools. He made it to a door and pushed himself up far enough so he could reach the door knob. He tried twisting it, but it wouldn't budge. He overheard people laughing and talking on the other side of the door. He didn't want to draw attention to himself but he didn't have much choice if he wanted to get out of their alive. He saw a window next to the door. He grabbed a brick that was in his grasp and laid down on the floor, aiming for the window. Once he knew for sure that he had a good shot, he threw his phone straight through the window. The glass shattered everywhere and he heard the chatter stop.

"Help," he yelled. He was hoping that the people heard him.

"Did you hear that, Bobby?" Sammy heard one voice ask.

"Yeah, I did, Larry. You think somebody is really in there?"

"Probably some kids playing a prank."

"Maybe we should go check it out," Larry said.

"I don't think so, pal. You can go ahead though."

Sammy listened. He could hear the two guys voices getting lower and lower.

They were leaving.

He yelled again but they never came back. He heard the stranger coming back. He grabbed Sammy by the arms and pulled him down the hall to the room he was in.

Now what am I gonna do? Sammy thought to himself. *Now what?*

Chapter Two:
Facing My Fears

Parker heard his alarm clock go off. He jumped out of the bed, remembering not to make too much noise, because he wasn't supposed to be here. He put his ear to his bedroom door. There wasn't any movement going on just yet on this bright Saturday morning. T   here hardly ever was, though; it was only 8 o'clock. He tiptoed downstairs, wearing the same clothes he had on the previous night. He went to the front door and opened and closed it. As he was trying to creep back up to his room, his mother startled him.

"You're back early, Parker," she replied. She was coming from the basement carrying a large hamper in her arms.

"Oh, yeah, hey, Mom. I, uh, got baseball practice this morning. Remember?" he said breathing heavily.

"That's right," she said, placing the hamper on the floor. "Well, you're gonna need this," she replied pulling out his baseball jersey and tossing it his way.

"Thanks, Mom."

"You're welcome, sweetheart. Would you like me to make you some oatmeal?" she yelled up the staircase.

"No, I'm okay," he yelled back to her. He quickly showered and dressed in his baseball gear. He opted to put his cleats in his backpack instead of wearing them out the house like he usually did. He ran back down the steps and saw his mom in the kitchen. He ran to give her a kiss and grabbed an apple out of the fruit basket. He locked the front door on his way out, hopped on his bike, and headed to the baseball field for practice.

He rode by Grady Hospital and stopped. He examined the building and all the crows that were lingering about.

"This place is so freaking creepy," he said aloud. He placed both feet back on the pedals and continued on.

✳✳✳✳

After another successful practice, it was time to head back home, but something didn't feel right to Parker. Sammy had missed practice this morning. He tried calling his cell phone, but got no answer. All he kept getting was his answering machine. He called three more times and the result was the same. As soon as he hung up, his phone began to ring. Without looking at the caller ID, he quickly answered.

"Hey, Sammy," he said happily.

"Sammy? Parker, this is Melody," she replied.

"Oh, hey, Melody. What are you doing?"

"Nothing. Patty and I are just sitting around watching the annual Halloween movie marathon. Why did you think I was Sammy? What's going on, Parker?" she said, placing the phone on speaker. She made sure to turn the volume down so her parents wouldn't overhear. She moved over to where Patty was and held the phone up so they could both hear.

"I don't really know, exactly. Sammy didn't show up for baseball practice today, and he's not answering his phone."

"Why didn't you call his parents and ask if they've seen him?" Melody asked.

"Why would he do that?" Patty chimed in. "He was supposed to be at Parker's house last night, remember?"

"Oh, yeah," Melody responded. "I forgot."

"You guys haven't heard anything from him?" Parker asked frantically.

"Nope," they both responded.

"I'm worried, you guys."

"What for?" Patty asked.

"Sammy is missing," Parker said in a sarcastic tone.

"Are you two that gullible? This is Sammy we're talking about. He pulls crap like this all the time."

"But what if this isn't a joke?" Melody asked.

"It is. And you two crybabies are gonna fall for his tricks, just like always," Patty said laughing.

"I doubt that it's a joke," Parker said, cutting off her laughter. "Sammy's my best friend, and I know him. He would have revealed himself by now."

"If you say so," Patty replied.

No Trespassing

"When was the last time you saw him, Parker?" Melody asked.

"Last night. I last saw him when we were running out of Grady."

"Same here," Melody replied.

"Likewise," Patty agreed.

"We need to meet up. Meet me back at the hospital later tonight," Parker said. "I have to go home and change clothes."

"If Sammy is missing, so you say, why would we wait until later, Parker? Does that make any sense to you?" Patty asked.

"I would say let's go now, but I don't want to make my parents suspicious. I'm gonna stay in for a while and go about my normal routine. I'm just gonna tell my folks that I'm staying at Sammy's house again tonight."

"That makes sense, I guess," Melody replied.

They all agreed to meet back at the hospital before hanging up. Melody and Patty got situated on their end while Parker did what he had to do.

✳✳✳✳

"So, what happened to you staying at Grady Hospital last night?" Marvin asked as he walked into Parker's room, uninvitingly, again.

Parker quickly jumped to his feet and ran to shut his bedroom door. He pushed Marvin over to the bed and told him to sit down. "Shut up, Marvin. We did go there last night."

"But you didn't stay. I saw you when you came in the house last night."

"You did? How? I was so careful."

"Don't worry about it. I didn't tell Mom and Dad."

"Are you going to?" Parker asked nervously.

"Nope. I just want to know why you chickened out," he said, laughing.

"Look, Marvin, something bad happened."

"Like what?"

"We kind of lost Sammy last night."

"You did what?" he said loudly. Parker immediately threw his hand over his brother's mouth. "Sorry," Marvin said, whispering. "How did you guys kind of lose Sammy, Parker?"

"I don't know, exactly. When we heard somebody coming we-"

"You guys heard somebody there? Did you see who it was?"

"No, but whoever it was grabbed Patty and-"

"Really? Holy cow. You have to-"

"Can you be quiet for a second, Marvin? *Geez.*" Marvin got quiet and continued to listen to his little brother's story. "Like I was saying, something or someone grabbed Patty. We all ran out of the hospital when we heard them coming towards us. I thought we were all together but we didn't find out until today that Sammy has been

M.I.A. We called and texted him. The only answer to where he could possibly be is the hospital."

"Can I talk now?" Marvin asked when Parker stopped talking. He nodded his head. "Well, I don't know what to say. Are you all sure that he isn't playing a prank?"

"That's the same thing Patty said."

"It could be possible."

"Yeah, it could be possible, but I highly doubt it. He's my best friend. He would have been gloating about it by now. Why would he even try to pull a cruel prank like this anyway? It doesn't make any logical sense."

Marvin thought about it for a few seconds. A light bulb went off in his head and he stood to his feet. "It is a prank, Parker. It's Halloween weekend. Oh, wow," Marvin said, laughing. "That's the only explanation."

Parker thought about it; that could have been a possibility. Every year, Sammy pulls a Halloween prank on him, but never has he pranked the girls, too, especially not Patty. She was the best prankster in the school. She got all of her master prank skills from her father, the original and best prankster of his time.

"I still don't believe that," Parker replied. "I think he's in trouble, I can just feel it. Especially since he didn't show up for baseball practice today. I think we're gonna still go and check it out, just to be on the safe side, you know?"

"Yeah, I understand. Sammy never misses baseball practice, at least to my knowledge. One thing I don't understand, though, is why didn't you just call his house if you couldn't get him on his cell phone?"

"Because he was supposed to have spent the night here last night. How would that look, if I called his parents house and asked for him? That would worry them and I would get busted by Mom and Dad. It's just too risky."

"That's true. They would freak if they knew what you had done."

"Are you gonna tell on me?"

"Oh, no. I'm gonna be in as much trouble as you if I squeal."

"You? Why you? You didn't do anything."

"Um, yeah, I kinda did. I was the one that said something about it and dared you to go there. In all honesty, though, I didn't think you were really gonna go. When you said that you were, I thought you were bluffing. I just knew you were gonna go over to Sammy's house and play games all night."

"Why, because I'm a wimp?"

"No, because you never lie to Mom and Dad about your whereabouts. You pulled that off better than I did the first time I lied to them about where I was going. I'm a little proud," Marvin said, laughing and wiping away an invisible tear. Parker just rolled his eyes at him. Their conversation was briefly interrupted by their mother.

"Hey, Parker-" she said opening the door after knocking. She paused when she saw Marvin in there as well. "What's going on now?" she asked with her arms folded.

No Trespassing

"Nothing, Mom," Marvin said. "We were just in here talking. That's all."

"Oh, really?" she asked. She looked over at Parker.

"Yeah, Mom. We're just talking."

"Mmhmm. About what?" she prodded.

"Just guy stuff," Marvin said, throwing an arm around Parker's neck and pulling him closer.

"I guess. Well dinner will be ready in five. Be downstairs, and no rough housing when I leave out this door."

"We'll be right down," Marvin replied. Their mother closed the door. They waited until they heard her going down the stairs before they continued their conversation. They decided to keep whispering, just to be on the safe side.

"Do you think she heard anything?" Parker asked Marvin.

"I doubt it. We weren't talking that loud. Mom's hearing isn't as good as it used to be. I wouldn't worry if I were you."

"I hope you're right. Getting in trouble and grounded is not on my to-do list."

"I can dig that, bro. I think we should get downstairs before she comes back up here to get us."

"I think so, too," Parker agreed.

No Trespassing

During dinner, the table was so quiet that you could hear a pin drop on the floor. All you could hear were the low voices coming from the newscasters on the television in the den, and the taps of the knives and forks as they hit the porcelain dinner plates. His mother had prepared his favorite meal. Mashed potatoes, broccoli, and boneless chicken breasts adorned his plate. Parker was trying to enjoy his favorite meal, but he didn't have an appetite tonight. He wanted to act as normal as possible, but right now his mind was elsewhere. His mind was on Sammy. He played with the broccoli on his fork as his mind wandered to unsettling thoughts about his friend.

"What's the matter, hun?" his mother, Elaine, asked her young son.

"Nothing, Mom. I'm okay."

"Oh, pish posh, Parker. Something is wrong. You have barely even touched your food."

"I just don't have an appetite tonight."

His mother placed her hand on his forehead. "Well, you don't feel warm."

"Hey, Mom, can I go over to Sammy's house tonight?"

"Again, Parker? You were just there last night."

"I know, but we have this Fortnite tournament going on," he lied.

"You can play from your room, Parker. You need to stay home and spend time with your family."

"I don't want to spend time with the family," Parker said, throwing his fork down.

"Pipe down, Parker," his father, Eliot, chimed in. "You will not use that tone of voice with your mother."

"All I wanna do is go and hangout with my friend," Parker yelled across the dinner table.

"That's it," his father said, throwing down his napkin and standing to his feet. He pointed his finger at Parker. "You are grounded, young man. Now go to your room, this instant."

Parker scooted his chair back across the hardwood floor and threw down his napkin. He mumbled under his breath as he stomped up the steps and headed to his room. No more than twenty minutes had gone by before he heard a light tap on the door and Marvin peeked his head in. Parker motioned for him to come in. Marvin closed the door quietly and sat on his brother's bed.

"So, what are you gonna do now, Park?' he asked in a whisper.

"I'm not gonna let that stop me. I'm still going."

"You're gonna disobey Mom and Dad? What has gotten into you, Parker?"

"Nothing has gotten into me, Marvin. I'm just trying to find my friend. What if he ends up like those people you were telling me about? What if Willie McNair got ahold of Sammy?"

"I don't know what else to tell you, little brother; it seems like your mind is made up. What time are you leaving?"

"As soon as Mom and Dad go to bed."

"Just be careful," Marvin told him.

"I will," Parker replied. As soon as Marvin left the room, Parker texted Patty and Melody and told them to meet him back at the hospital around 10:30. They both agreed that they would sneak out and be there.

Parker decided that he would probably need some artillery if he wanted to get Sammy out safely. He grabbed his backpack and made sure his flashlight was still in there. He heard footsteps coming up the steps. He heard the light taps on his door. He quickly threw the bag under his bed and stretched out on top. His parents peeped through the door to check on him. Once they confirmed that he was okay, and was about to go to sleep, they said their goodnights to one another and they left back out.

 As soon as he heard their room door shut down the hall, he jumped back up. He pulled the bag from under his bed. Gently, he opened his window and, as quiet as a prowler, he descended the built-in ladder and headed to the tool shed around back. He opened it, and the door creaked. He was glad his parents' room was on the front side of the house rather than the back side like Marvin's. Parker went inside the shed and closed the door as soon as he turned the light on. Their father had so much stuff in here that he used for hunting. He grabbed some rope, just in case he had to tie up the person that may have taken Sammy hostage. He looked around to see what other supplies he could possibly use. His eyes fell onto a Philips screwdriver. He picked it up and swung it.

"This will work," he said aloud. He continued to look. He knew that Melody and Patty were gonna need something to protect themselves, as well. He saw a crowbar lying on the workbench.

"Patty would love to use this. I'm sure of it," he said, placing it in his backpack with the crowbar. He grabbed two flashlights out of the emergency kit that their father had made in case of a tornado or hurricane. Parker was still unsure of why his father had this; they never had natural disasters in Denver, Colorado. After gathering up his supplies, Parker checked his watch. It was 9:30. His parents still weren't asleep, he knew that for a fact. He climbed back up to his room and sat the bag behind his door. He laid down on his bed and tried his best to patiently wait for his parents to fall asleep for the night.

✳✳✳✳

It was finally a quarter after 10 when Parker could hear his dad snoring from down the hall. It never ceased to amaze him how his mother could sleep through that loud and obnoxious snoring every night. He didn't really have time to ponder this thought, since he was on a mission.

] He got up and grabbed his bag of supplies. He went to turn off his table lamp when he noticed his baseball bat in the corner. He thought for a second before grabbing that as well and stuffing it into his backpack. He scaled down the side of the house like Spider-man and grabbed his bike from the side of the house. Just as he placed his foot on the pedal, and was ready to push off with the other, somebody tapped his shoulder.

"*Aahhh!*" he screamed. The person put a tight hand over his mouth.

"*Shhhhh.* Are you trying to get us busted?" Marvin whispered into his ear and released his mouth.

"Are you trying to give me a heart attack? What are you doing snooping around out here, Marvin?"

"I was in my room thinking, and I wanna go help you find Sammy."

"Why? You don't even like Sammy."

"That is a true statement, but I can't help but to think this is partially my fault."

"Partially?"

"Hey, that's all you get, squirt. I'm coming with you. Let me grab my bike," Marvin said, disappearing to the back of the house. He came back moments later. "What's wrong?" he asked Parker when he noticed him staring.

"If you're going, why not just take your car? We would get there quicker."

"Yeah, and it will also be very noticeable. Everybody in this town knows my car. I don't wanna be grounded along with you. Sorry, bro, but I have a date for Halloween tomorrow with Macy Crenshaw."

"That cheerleader I overheard you and your butthead friend talking about on the phone?"

"The one and only," he said with a big grin.

"Ew, gross," Parker replied.

"You will be like this one day, Parker, so cut it out."

"Whatever, Marvin. Let's just go before Willie McNair starts to feast on Sammy's skull or something."

"Lead the way, master," Marvin said. Parker shook his head before heading away from the house as quietly and as quickly as possible, with his brother riding behind him closely.

****

"It took you long enough to get here, Parker," Melody said with her hands on her hips.

"And what is Marvin doing here?" Patty asked as she scrunched her face up when she saw him approaching.

"He's here to help," Parker said, leaning his bike onto the gate.

"Yeah, I bet," Melody responded.

"What?" Marvin asked defensively. "I'm just trying to help Parker and you girls find Sammy."

"How do you know he's not pranking us with Sammy, Parker? They could have been in cahoots this entire time," Melody said.

"I don't think that's possible. They can't stand each other, so there is no way they would work together."

"Are you sure Sammy is here, Parker?" Patty asked, exasperated as they stood outside the hospital's gate.

"Where else could he possibly be, Pat?"

"I don't know, but I definitely don't think we should go back in there. Especially after what happened last night."

"I agree with Patty," Melody said.

"Are you really scared, Patty? I thought you were tough."

"I am tough, Parker, but there is a big difference between being tough and being stupid. We are smart people, and smart people would not go back into a dangerous situation."

"Doesn't seem like it to me," Marvin said, laughing. "Maybe you little girls should run on home. Leave this to real men," he said, punching Parker in the shoulder.

"Oh, be quiet, Marvin. If you had never dared Parker to come here in the first place, we wouldn't be in this mess," Patty yelled.

"Hey, don't blame me for this. I didn't think the little twerp was gonna actually do it," Marvin said.

"Calm down, Pat. We don't wanna draw any attention to ourselves," Parker said to her.

"Why don't we just call the cops?" Melody suggested.

"And tell them what, Mel?" Parker asked sarcastically. "Hey, 911, we have an emergency. We broke into the abandoned hospital last night. Even though it had a big sign that read 'no trespassing', we didn't listen and went inside anyway. Something grabbed one of our friends and we all ran out. Only thing I forgot to mention though, one of our friends are missing now. Is that what you wanna tell them, Melody?" he yelled.

"Don't yell at me, Parker. This is all your fault anyway! I told you it was a bad idea from the jump, but did you listen? No!"

"All three of y'all need to take a chill pill," Marvin exclaimed as he got off his bike and leaned it against the gate. You all are upset, scared, and acting crazy. I can understand that, but you all going back and forth arguing is not gonna help find Sammy any sooner. Just relax. We cannot go in there with our heads all over the place. We do need to hurry up, though, before Willie chops up Sammy."

"Marvin's right, you guys. Well as far as us needing to calm down. Definitely not the chopping up Sammy part," Parker uttered as he gave Marvin a crazy look. "We need to settle down and get our minds right. We need to be on the same team right now."

"I know Sammy is our friend and all but, I just want to go home. I don't wanna be here at all. This is dangerous you guys. And what if we go in here and Sammy's not here? What if Willie whatever his name has decomposed Sammy's body and waiting for us to come back?" Melody rambled.

"Wow, you have a very active imagination, Melody," Marvin said, clapping.

"Oh, shut your piehole, Marvin," Melody snapped at him.

"Look, Mel, we can argue back and forth until the sun comes up, but at the end of the day no matter how much of a chicken I may be, I have to go in there and at least see if my best friend needs my help. Now, are you coming or not?" Parker asked.

She looked Marvin's way and rolled her eyes at him. He just snickered at her. She then looked back and forth between Parker and Patty before reluctantly telling them yes.

They all gathered together and were walking to the steps when Patty stepped on something hard. She shrieked at the crackling sound. She jumped behind Parker and he turned his flashlight on.

"It's Sammy's cell phone," he said, picking it up and examining it closer.

"Is that blood on it?" Melody asked in a trembling voice. Tears from fear started to form in her eyes.

"Looks like it," Parker replied.

"I was hoping you weren't gonna say that," Patty said.

"Let me see that," Marvin said, taking the phone out of his brother's hand. "This blood is still a little fresh."

"What does that mean?" Melody asked in a panic.

"It means Sammy is in trouble and he needs our help," Parker responded.

"See, I am so out of here," Melody said walking back out of the gate. She made it to the corner before the others caught up to her.

"Where are you going, Melody?" Patty asked, grabbing her by the arm.

"I'm getting out of here, Patty," she replied as the tears started to stream down her face. "And if you all had brains you would leave, too."

"You can't just leave, Mel," Parker said.

"Oh? And why not? Because you want to prove yourself?"

"Not only that, but I want to help my friend. My best friend."

"That is such crap, Parker, and you know it. Sammy is gone and we cannot change that," she said as she started to cry hysterically.

"You don't know that for sure, Melody," Parker said, pushing Patty out the way and grabbing Melody by both of her elbows.

"Let me go, Parker," she said, trying to wiggle out of his grip.

"Not until you think more rationally. This isn't just my fault and it isn't just Marvin's fault. We all came here, as a group, and none of us checked to make sure we left this place together. You need to get yourself together and get your head on your shoulders. We are *not* leaving here again without Sammy; I refuse to. Now, if you wanna leave, then leave. We don't need you here if you don't wanna be here," Parker said angrily as he released his hold on Melody and pushed her away. Luckily, Marvin was there to catch her from hitting the ground when she stumbled backwards. Parker walked back to the abandoned hospital, grabbing a flashlight out of his bag.

"Are you okay, Melody?" Patty asked hugging her friend.

"No, I'm not. I'm upset, and hurt right now. I have never seen Parker act like this before; especially not towards me."

"Yeah, I know what you mean," Marvin agreed. "Parker's under a lot of pressure right now. On top of him not knowing if Sammy's okay, I think he has finally reached his breaking point with people walking all over him."

"Fine time to reach a breaking point," Patty said, sucking her teeth.

"Exactly," Melody agreed. "And I don't have anything to do with that. I have never walked over Parker, and I never plan to do so. He has really lost his cool. I'm just so confused right now."

Just as they silenced their conversation, they noticed Parker walking back, carrying the backpack of supplies. He sat the bag down on the ground between them.

"What's in the bag, bro?" Marvin asked.

"Supplies," he said bluntly. He looked at Melody. "Look, I'm sorry how I acted a few minutes ago. It's just that I thought we were all friends, and we're supposed to look out for one another."

"We are friends, Parker. You know that," Melody said, sniffling and wiping her face.

"So, are you in or not?"

"I'm in," she replied hesitantly.

Parker gave both Patty and Marvin a flashlight. He handed Melody hers and hugged her tightly. As he was pulling away, he paused and kissed her on the cheek. Without making eye contact with her, he squatted back down into his bag. Melody stood there in awe. Patty looked on as a smile crept upon her best friend's face. Marvin pulled the neckline of his t-shirt over his mouth and smiled.

"I think we need a plan," Melody said, squatting down to eye level with Parker.

"That's not a bad idea," he said, looking into her blue eyes. She smiled.

"Hey, lovebirds, can we get this show on the road?" Marvin said, interrupting their staring contest. "It's already after midnight. That means we don't have much time before the sun comes up. Also, don't forget dad is knocking this place down as soon as the sun rises."

"He's right, you guys. That is a big building and there's no telling where Sammy could be if he's still alive," Patty chimed in.

"There is no 'if'," Parker said, standing back up. "He is still alive. I'm sticking to that until I am proven otherwise."

No Trespassing

"Way to stay positive, Park," Marvin said, slapping a hand on his brother's back.

"So, what's the plan, Parker?" Melody asked.

"Well, like I said, we have no choice but to go in there and find Sammy."

"No, duh, Parker," Patty said, rolling her eyes.

"My only thing is: what if that guy, Wilbur McNair, is still inside?" Melody asked.

"It's Willie McNair," Marvin chuckled.

"Who cares?" Melody shot back.

"I doubt he's inside, Mel," Parker said. "This place is abandoned, remember?"

"Yeah, Melody," Patty agreed.

"You guys cannot say that. We thought that yesterday, too, and looked what happened."

"That could've been a rat or something," Marvin asked.

"Rats don't have big hands, Marvin," Melody said, placing her hands firmly on her hips.

"*Geez*, can you two just quit it?" Parker yelled. "Melody, maybe it was a rat. Maybe it was a person. Or, maybe it was just all in your imagination. Who's to say exactly what that was? All I know is that I am not leaving here without Sammy, and that's final."

No Trespassing

"Don't you raise your voice at me, Parker Wilson," Melody yelled back at him.

"Sorry, Mel. I'm just getting frustrated."

"Does it look like I care about your frustration? That is no excuse to be rude and disrespectful to us; especially when going in there was your bright idea anyway."

"It was originally Sam and Pat's idea."

"Hey, don't put me in this," Patty said in defense.

"Well it was," Parker replied with a shrug of his shoulders.

"Doesn't matter, Parker," Melody said, pointing at him. "it was your idea to come back here. If it wasn't for you and your lack of self-confidence, we wouldn't even be in this mess, and Sammy would definitely not be missing." A brush of silence fell over them as they looked at each other with guilty stares. "Look, I'm sorry, but it needed to be said."

"I'm glad you look it at that way," Parker said, walking away. Melody grabbed him by the arm and stopped him in his tracks.

"I didn't mean it like that, Parker. I told you before, you don't have to prove how brave you are by doing something as stupid as this. It was dangerous coming here the first time, and now, because of this stupid idea, one of our friends are missing. I'm hoping he is in here. Did you even think this through before you decided to come the first time?"

"No," Parker replied, lowering his eyes to the ground.

"Exactly my point. Like I said before, if you were thinking rationally, we wouldn't be in this predicament. All in all, it doesn't matter who's fault it is. The only thing that should be on our minds is the fact that Sammy is missing. Right now is not the time to be playing the blame game. We need to find Sammy and get him, and ourselves, out of here in one piece. Okay?"

"Okay," they all said in unison.

"Wait," Patty said. "What are we gonna do about protection?"

Parker reached into his bag and gave Patty the crowbar. She whacked her hand with it to test its durability. He handed the baseball bat to Melody and she gladly accepted it. He grabbed the screwdriver and pushed it deep into his pocket. "Is everybody ready?" he asked. The two girls nodded their heads and they headed back to the hospital.

"Whoa, whoa, whoa. What about me?" Marvin asked.

"You have to get your own weapon. I didn't pack enough for four people, only three. Sorry, bro."

"That is selfish, Parker," Marvin said as he looked around until he saw a loose pole hanging from the gate. He went over and jiggled it until it came apart. "I'm ready now."

The four walked back up to the gate and stood there once again. They were as ready as they would ever be. They all took a deep breath. They all turned on their flashlights as they headed inside the abandoned hospital for the second night in a row.

Chapter Three:
Search and Rescue

"It smells more awful in here than the last time," Melody said, covering her nose with her sweater.

"It smells the same to me," Parker said, shrugging his shoulders. He flicked on his flashlight and the others followed in tow.

"Wow this is sick," Marvin said, scanning the room with his flashlight.

"It does smell worse than before," Patty said, walking closer to the group.

They were standing near the receptionist desk as they looked around at the many rooms that lined the dark hallway.

"Where should we check first?" Marvin asked Parker.

"Not sure, honestly. Let's look over there first, I guess," he said, pointing into the darkness. The others followed behind him as he headed towards one of the rooms. They walked into the room that had a number 13 outside of the door.

"Stop walking so fast, Parker," Melody said. She walked a little quicker to catch up to him. She grabbed his arm and locked it in hers. She was determined not to let him go or leave his side by any means.

"Would you look at this mess?" Patty said. She was shining her flashlight across a bed. She pulled the corner of the sheet and examined it. There were blood stains splotched all over it. She dropped it as soon as she saw cockroaches and ants crawling on the underside of it. She placed her flashlight on the bed again and scanned it all the way up to the pillows. There were more splotches of blood along with hair strands and maggots. The hair strands looked as though they were ripped right out of someone's scalp the way they appeared.

"This place is gross."

"Tell me about," Melody said. She was standing between Parker and Marvin as they searched through hospital cabinets. "What are you guys looking for, Parker?" she asked.

"I don't know. I guess clues about what happened here," I responded.

"I thought we were looking for Sammy?"

"We can do both, Mel," Marvin responded.

"Don't call me that, Marvin."

"Lighten up," he replied back.

"I will not lighten up. We need to do what we came here to do. If you guys are gonna be in here trying to find clues to an unsolved mystery, count me out. I did not come here for this," Melody said, stomping her foot.

"Calm down, Mel," Patty said, walking over to her. She grabbed her by her arms. "Look, we are going to find Sammy, okay? It wouldn't hurt to know what happened here."

"I guess," she said.

"Or, you can just leave if you don't want to be here, Melody," Marvin chimed in.

"Who asked you? If you think I'm walking out of here this time of night by myself, you're crazier than I thought," she said, rolling her eyes at him.

"I was joking," he laughed.

"But I wasn't," she shot back.

"Hey, guys, look what I found," Parker said, momentarily breaking up their feud. They walked over to where he was. They surrounded him as he shined his light inside of a closet that was behind the hospital room door.

"Is that a bloody axe?" Melody asked with a quivering voice.

"Yeah, I think it is," Parker replied, reaching for it.

"Don't touch it!" Patty yelled as she grabbed his arm and pulled it back.

"Why not?" he and Marvin said simultaneously.

"Because it might have some disease or something on it."

"I highly doubt that," Marvin said.

"Well I don't," she replied, folding her arms across her chest.

"I don't doubt that either, Marvin," Melody said. "Even though you don't think it does, you could be wrong."

"Well, if it's been here for 45 years, I don't believe that a disease or whatever would still be on it. There is no possible way that there could be."

"Well, do what you want," Melody replied. "Don't cry to me when your hand falls off or catches an infection and needs to be cut off," she walked back over to the other side of the room.

"Me neither," Patty said, walking away and joining Melody.

"What about you, Parker? You're with your big brother, right?"

"Sorry, Bro. I like both of my hands right where they are."

"You guys are a bunch of wimps."

"Call us what you want," Patty said. "At least we won't have to worry about having to get our hands chopped off, or something if it gets infected."

"Just from one touch? You little kids are silly," Marvin said, waving them away.

"Okay, don't believe us. Don't say we didn't warn you," Melody said as she and Patty peered out the window.

Marvin moved his flashlight back across the axe again. *On second thought, I better not,* he thought to himself.

"What are you guys looking at?" Parker asked Melody and Patty as he joined them at the window.

"Nothing, really. Just looking outside for comfort, wishing we were out there. Well, at home in our beds, anyway," Melody said, looking at her watch and seeing that the time was nearing 1 a.m. "It's getting late, you guys. We need to find Sammy, and fast."

"She's right," Patty said in agreement. "It's 12:55 in the morning and we haven't even began our search. We have to stop fooling around and I mean now."

"You're both right. The demolition is gonna probably be here right at the crack of dawn. Come on, guys," Parker said, leading them back into the lobby. "Patty, you check that room," he pointed to the room next to the one they just exited. "Marvin, you check that room. Melody, you can look in there, and I will look over there. Make sure to look around thoroughly for Sammy and we will meet back here in about ten, maybe fifteen, minutes." Without any arguments, the four went into their designated room in search of Sammy.

Patty walked over to room 14 with her flashlight illuminating the way for her. She pushed on the heavy door and listened to the spine-tingling creaking as it opened all the way. It hit the wall behind it and she slowly entered the room. There were two beds in here; they were flipped over, and so were a few crash carts that doctors used to revive people. Using her flashlight, she walked further into the room. She moved the door and checked the closet for Sammy first. She opened the door but nothing was there but some clothes hanging up, and some cobwebs. She closed it again and walked over to the bathroom. The same as the closet, nothing was there.

"This is such a waste," she said aloud to herself. She walked over to look on the other side of the beds. As soon as she walked past the first bed, laying on the floor was a skeleton. It was brown and covered in cobwebs and worms were playing through its bones. She quickly ran out of the room and ran into room 11 where Patty was.

No Trespassing

"*Aahhh!*" Melody screamed when Patty grabbed her from behind. She swung her fists and accidently hit Patty in the chin.

"What was that for?" Patty yelled, grabbing her chin.

"Are you crazy, Pat? Why on earth would you scare me like that? Are you just trying to give me a heart attack?"

"No, sorry. I didn't mean to but I got scared."

"Scared of what, Patty?" Melody asked as she paused.

"I found a skeleton in the room."

"Really, Pat? A skeleton? You almost killed your best friend over a bag of bones?" she asked sarcastically before bursting into laughter. After thinking it through, Patty realized that it was ridiculous and joined Melody in laughter.

"I don't care what you say, I'm not going back in there. I'm staying right here with you, Mel."

"Cool beans," she replied.

"Have you found anything that might lead us to Sammy yet?"

"Nope. The only place I haven't checked was the bathroom and the closet."

"Well, I will check it with you, then." The two girls walked close together as they entered the bathroom first. As they both used their flashlights, they saw that there were no clues there, so they headed over to the closet.

"Oh, my goodness," Patty said as soon as their lights flashed into the closet.

No Trespassing

"Is that Sammy's hat?" Melody asked, stammering over her words.

Patty knelt down to retrieve the hat. After careful examination, she concluded that it was indeed the hat that Sammy wore every day. "We need to show this to Parker and Marvin."

"Let's go." As soon as they left out of the room, Parker was coming out of room 7 and heading back to the receptionist desk. A few feet behind him, Marvin was emerging from room nine.

"Did you guys find anything?" Parker asked the girls.

"We found Sammy's hat," Melody replied, crying.

"What's the matter?" Parker said, running over to comfort her.

"I'm just so scared. This place is giving me the creeps, and we still haven't found Sammy," she said, crying on his shoulder.

"Calm down," he said. "We're gonna find him and we're all gonna get out of here together, okay?"

She nodded her head.

"I found an old skeleton," Patty said.

"You sure it wasn't Sammy?" Marvin asked, laughing. They all looked at him with disgusted stares.

"That's not funny, you jerk," Melody spazzed.

"Exactly. Besides, the bones were old and worn. Plus, it looked to be the remains of an adult, not a kid."

"Maybe it was Willie McNair," Marvin replied.

"Maybe," Parker said. "I don't care who's remains they are. As long as they aren't Sammy's, I couldn't care less."

"Well, what do we do now?" Patty asked everybody.

"We can either start at the top and work our way downstairs, or we can continue to search on this floor, or we can all just go down to the basement," Parker said.

"After Patty said she saw that skeleton, and then us finding Sammy's hat, I don't wanna check anywhere else. Who knows what we may find next?" Melody cried.

"We are all gonna be here with each other. Nothing is going to happen to you if we all stick together," Parker reassured her.

"Since this is an abandoned hospital, where there was a legendary massacre, I'm sure we will find a lot of stuff," Marvin stated. "Blood, more dead bodies, maybe severed heads, and-"

"Marvin!" Parker yelled. "Chill out with all of that. You're scaring everybody."

"Sheesh, Parker, who scraped the icing off your cupcake? Honestly, I don't know whose more of a chicken between the three of you."

"Hey, I'm not a chicken," Patty said defensively.

"Yeah, you're right, Patty. Then, between Parker and Melody, I'm not sure whose worse."

"Shut up, Marvin," Parker said, balling his fists up and staring Marvin down with an angry glare.

No Trespassing

"Oh, pipe down, Parker. You have gotten a little beside yourself with this whole standing up for yourself charade and whatnot. I'm proud that you found that little ounce of bravery inside of yourself, and you're using it to prance up and down this abandoned hospital searching for Sammy, but do not, I repeat, do not, let these fifteen minutes of confidence be the reason you catch a beatdown. I'm your brother and I know you better than any one of your little friends. I can see right through you. You're trying to fake like you're brave just so we can stay here with you all night. I bet if we were to leave right now you would leave out, too. And then say forget about Sammy. You know why? Because you're a big chicken. A wimp. A crybaby. Anything that revolves around the word punk, reflects you. And there's nothing you can do to change who you are," Marvin said, folding his arms across his chest as smiling.

Parker could see his bright white teeth in the dark space and it infuriated him more. The brothers stared each other down as the two girls became onlookers of the situation that was sure to erupt. In a blink of an eye, Patty and Melody watched as Parker ran towards Marvin and knocked him off his feet. The two slid across the floor, just barely hitting the automatic sliding glass door. "Get off of me, you little brat," Marvin replied as Parker grabbed him by the collar of his flannel shirt.

"I am so sick of you, Marvin," Parker yelled at the top of his lungs as he slammed his brother's head onto the tiled floor.

"I said get off of me, Parker," Marvin yelled back. He managed to get Parker's grip off of his shirt and he pushed him off top of him. He sat up and Parker came back again. The two brothers wrestled and tousled around on the cold, hard, and mildew flooring and didn't think twice about it.

"Shouldn't we be breaking this fight up?" Melody asked in a panic.

No Trespassing

"Oh, no, Mel. I have been waiting years to see Parker fight somebody,and just so happens, it's Marvin. This day had come sooner than I had expected and I am not disappointed," Patty laughed as she egged on the fight. She even pulled out her cell phone to take a video.

"This is ridiculous. Break it up you two," Melody said, walking over to the fighting siblings. She tried pulling Marvin off of Parker, but she couldn't. She wasn't strong enough. She tried pulling Parker's hand from his brother's neck. Again, she was too weak to break them apart. "Patty are you gonna just stand there and record or are you gonna help me?"

"Gee, Mel, I would love to, but this fight is gold. Who would have ever thought that one day Parker Wilson would go berserk and spaz on his own brother? And, luckily for me, I won't miss a moment of it," she said, laughing.

"Patty!" Melody shrieked. Patty knew Melody was getting irritated by her behavior.

"Fine, fine," Patty said, putting her phone back into her pocket. She went over and they both used all of their strength to pull Marvin off of Parker. Once they got a good hold of him, they drug him across the room and away from Parker. As they had finally got them separated, the boys were both staring one another down from across the room.

"Just so you know, it doesn't matter how many nights you stay in this place, Parker. You will always be a loser. A big cry baby loser. How could someone as cool as me have such a dorky brother like you?" Marvin said, wiping sweat from his forehead.

"You have some nerve talking about me, Marvin," Parker uttered. "You can call me all the names you want. You can call me a doofus, a cry baby, a wimp, whatever, but, you know what you can't call me? *Dumb*. You, on the other hand, I can call dumb," Parker said with a smirk on his face.

"Dumb? Who are you calling dumb, Parker?"

"I'm guessing the only person in this room that had to repeat second grade twice. I mean, *wow*. What kind of idiot flunks second grade? There is nothing to do but read and turn in your completed homework," Parker said, laughing hysterically.

"I got you, wise guy," Marvin said. He charged back towards his little brother. He ran right through Melody and Patty, bumping their shoulders hard as he made his way to Parker.

Once he grabbed a hold of him, he grabbed him by the shirt and threw him against the glass door. The entire door shattered, and glass flew all around them. Afraid they may get cut because they couldn't see where it had gone in the dark, the girls never moved a muscle. Melody used her flashlight and noticed that none of the glass had come near her or Patty. *What a relief.* Even the fact that glass probably cut them, or maybe even gotten into their skin, the boys disregarded it; their adrenaline was currently going through the roof as they managed to knock over a heart monitoring machine in the surgery area.

Marvin and Parker tousled all the way into one of the open room doors. Avoiding the glass doors this time, Marvin grabbed his brother by the shoulders. He spun him around and used his foot to kick Parker in the butt, sending him flying across the room. He fell into the hard wall and hit his mouth. He could feel the blood trickling from his nose and mouth as it made its way down to his shirt and stained it. Parker quickly became even more enraged by the sight of the blood. He rushed Marvin, and pushed him all the way out of the room, and into the nurses' desk. He jumped on Marvin and caused him to fall backwards behind the desk. It seemed as if there wasn't gonna be no ending to this fight.

Melody and Patty ran over to watch as the battle between the two siblings continued. Parker grabbed the base of the phone and hit Marvin in the face with it. Melody's hands flew over her mouth as she watched as Marvin's face was becoming red and slightly swollen from the impact of the phone's base. Patty, on the other hand, she had pulled her phone back out and start recording again. She continued to cheer on both parties and instigate the match. She pondered the thought and wondered who was gonna win the fight between the two.

"This is so stupid and childish," Melody yelled over the commotion. She might as well had been invisible because nobody was listening to her. Parker and his brother were too busy knocking over more stuff and destroying what property was left standing after the massacre. Patty wasn't any better. She was just full of laughs and grins as she enjoyed the show before her. Melody grabbed her flashlight and looked around the room. She was looking for something heavy to make a loud enough noise to stop Parker and Marvin. Her eyes fell on a brick, lying over in the corner, a few feet away from her. She walked fast over to it and picked it up. She quickly thought about what to do next.

I could slam the brick on the desk, she thought. *No, that won't work. My clumsy butt will probably end up smashing my little fingers.* She decided against that idea. She quickly found another way. She looked towards the sliding glass door. Stepping away from the commotion, she walked closer to the room that Marvin and Parker were previously wrestling in. She locked in her target and aimed. As hard as she

No Trespassing

could, she threw the brick through the glass. She dove onto the floor and covered as much of her head and face that she could with her arms. The glass went flying everywhere, even on Patty. But it worked.

The fighting had ceased.

I guess the glass startled them, Melody thought to herself.

"Hey, what gives?" Patty said, stopping her video and putting her phone into her pocket once again. She knocked the shattered glass from the sleeves of her sweatshirt and out of her hair.

"There is no 'what gives', Patty. I asked you to help me stop this madness, but instead you're standing here recording it like it's a Pay-Per-View match or something." Melody replied. She walked over to where Parker and Marvin were now standing. "And you two. You guys should be ashamed of yourselves. Y'all are supposed to be brothers, and y'all are acting like complete fools! I am so disappointed in you both, especially you, Parker."

"He started it," Parker said, pointing to Marvin.

"You sound like your tattling on me to Mom," Marvin said, wiping the blood from the side of his face. "And Melody, you need to calm down. You're overreacting."

"I don't wanna hear that, Marvin. Look at the two of you. You are supposed to be here to help us find our friend, but instead, you and Parker want to act like buffoons. "

"She's right," Parker said through swollen lips. "Let's try to find a first aid kit and clean ourselves up."

They all looked through the drawers until they found the white box. Patty and Melody cleaned and nursed Parker and Marvin's wounds as if they were professionals. Once they finished, the bickering between the two boys began again.

"I kicked your butt, Parker," Marvin replied.

"On top of being stupid, are you also delusional? I know you don't really think for a second that you beat me, Marvin. I think you need to use the few brain cells you have left and rethink that theory."

"Oh no, little brother, I think you are the delusional one. You think that just because you hit me with a couple of little baby punches and that phone that you actually did something? I think not," Marvin said, laughing.

"So, how about a rematch then?" Parker asked, jumping down from off top of the desk and stepping into Marvin's face.

"Come on, Bro," Marvin said, moving him out the way with his arm. Parker smacked it out of the way and stood in front of Marvin again. "Parker, come on now. You don't wanna get hurt anymore. Trust me, you don't. What's gonna happen when we go home and Mom and Dad see us like this? Questions are gonna be asked, and you're not gonna hold up. You're gonna be singing like a canary and we'll both be in deep dog poop."

"I'm not listening to anything you say. All I want to hear you say is that you want to have a rematch," Parker said, pushing Marvin in the chest. Marvin hopped down and stood toe to toe with his little brother. Looking up to meet his brother's gaze, Parker stared at him and made it known that he was not backing down.

"Cut it out, guys," Patty said, walking over to them. She squeezed between them enough to separate them, at least out of each other's arm reach anyway. "This is nonsense just like Melody said and you two need to stop it. How is any of this helping us find Sammy?"

"Exactly," Melody butted in. "And look what time it is? It's a quarter after two in the morning already and we have wasted unnecessary time. Time that could have and should have been used in looking for Sammy. You two need to grow up," she said, pointing her finger back and forth between Marvin and Parker.

"All I know is that with this newfound bravery, you are becoming idiotic," Marvin said, talking across Patty.

"You're idiotic, Marvin. I love my newfound bravery," Parker yelled, pounding his chest with his fist as if he were a gorilla.

"I hear ya, Parker, But how much bravery did you find inside yourself? Is it just enough to prance through this abandoned building to find your best friend? Or, did you build up enough to escape Willie McNair if he happens to pop up?"

"Oh, will you hush up about that crazy story?" Melody snapped. "I'm starting to believe that you just made it all up."

"And why on earth would I make up such a horrid story?" Marvin asked.

"To scare us. Well, to scare Parker anyway.

"Trust me when I tell you this, Melody: Parker doesn't need neither my help, nor your help, to be scared of anything. He was born with that trait," Marvin doubled over in laughter.

Patty flashed her light onto Parker's face. His face was all balled up and his eye was twitching; Melody looked and saw it as well. It frightened them both, because they had never seen their best friend like this. It looked as if a demon was slowly taking over his body.

Melody moved closer to Patty and pulled her from between Marvin and Parker. They stepped safely to the other side of the nurses' station and out of the way. They didn't know what was getting ready to transpire. They watched on as Parker's hands formed into fists once again. His arms were shaking from frustration and anger, and both were written all over his face. He landed two punches to Marvin's face before Marvin grabbed him by the neck. He picked him up by his throat and slammed him onto the desk. Parker screamed out in agonizing pain as he rolled of the desk and onto the floor. Marvin went to the side of the desk where Parker was and placed his foot on the side of his face. He leaned forward and put a little more pressure on his face. It was just enough to make him cry, but not enough to kill him.

"Get off of him," Patty yelled as she ran and tackled Marvin to the ground. Melody ran to Parker's side and helped him to his feet. "Stop this, Marvin. You, too, Parker."

"I don't think so, Pat. It's not as easy as you're trying to make it seem," Parker replied before knocking Marvin back to the ground after he had already struggled to make it to his feet.

Patty just threw her hands up in the air, finally deciding to give up. "Can you believe this?"

"You have some nerve," Melody said. "You were a part of this, too."

"Uh-uh, Mel. You will not say that." The girls just continued to watch and wondered when this pointless fight was going to end once and for all.

"What was that?" Patty asked Melody.

"What was what?" Melody asked.

"Shhh. Just listen." They listened closely to whatever it was that was trying to drown out the noise from Parker and Marvin. Patty looked to where the sound had come from. "Oh, false alarm," she said placing a hand on her chest. "It's just the creaking of the stairs from the wind."

"How do you know it's from the wind?"

"Look," Patty said as she pointed out the broken window. They watched as the dead tree branches hit up against the doors and windows. They both let out a nervous laugh, but their laughter was cut short.

Out of nowhere, they heard loud screams far in the distance. It was so loud that it caused Parker and Marvin to stop their Royal Rumble match. They stood on their feet and adjusted their clothes.

"Did you all hear that?" Melody asked. They all remained quiet and listened again.

"*Aahhh!*" the voice said again. Only this time, it echoed.

"There it is again. Did y'all hear it again that time, or is it just my imagination running wild?"

"Yeah," they all said in unison.

"We heard it both times, Melody," Parker said as he wiped a little bit of the excess dust from his clothing.

"Where did that scream just come from?" Marvin asked.

"Who knows?" Patty asked. "This place is humongous. It's hard to say exactly where it may have come from. All I know is that it sounded a little like Sammy screaming."

"If that was Sammy, then that means he's still alive," Melody said, finally cracking a smile.

"That's good news, right?" Patty asked, looking around at everybody.

"Yeah. It's awesome news," Parker said to her.

"So, what do we do now?" Patty asked.

"Well, there is only one thing we can do. We're gonna have to split up," Parker said to her.

"Split up? Is your noodle loose? Do we look like Scooby and Shaggy?" Patty interrupted.
Everybody couldn't help but laugh.

"That's the only way we're gonna be able to cover more ground, Patty. There is no way we're gonna be able to stick together and search every inch of this hospital."

"We could if we try," Patty interjected again.

"Not a chance," Marvin said. "Splitting up is the only option."

"This is insane. Do you agree with this too, Melody?"

"I mean, the hospital is big, Pat. We should be able to find Sammy within a reasonable time if we split up in pairs. I don't see anything wrong with that. We can split up into teams and whoever finds Sammy will call the other two. We could all be walking out of here before sunrise. Whatever we do, we need to hurry. I don't wanna get caught by Parker's dad. My parents will have my head."

"As will ours," Parker said in agreement. "I had to sneak out tonight because I told my mother I wanted to go over Sammy's house. She told me no, but I had no choice. So, therefore, I am going to find him and I'm not leaving here without him again. Does everybody understand?"

"Yes," they all said in unison.

"Now, back to the plan. Marvin, you take the basement. Patty, you take the second level. Melody, you can take the main level and I will check the top floor. Any questions?"

"Why are we splitting up into individuals, Parker? Why can't we just go in pairs?" Melody asked.

"Because, Melody, we can cover more ground that way."

"How will we stay in contact with one another if we get lost or something?" Melody asked.

"We're gonna use our cell phones, like you just said. Any more questions?"

"Yeah," Marvin said, raising his hand into the air. "Why do I have to go down into the basement? Why one of the girls can't go? Or you?"

"Are you kidding me? I will not go into anybody's basement with these Prada shoes on," Melody said.

"Seriously? I don't know what's worse right now: this plan Parker just came up with, or the fact that you opted to wear those instead of sneakers like a normal person."

"Knock it off, guys," Parker said, breaking up the back and forth. "Now, is everybody okay with the plan?"

"Not like we have much of a choice," Patty said.

"Okay then. We have roughly three hours to find Sammy and get out of here before my dad's demolition begins. So, please, no fooling around people."

They all wished each other luck and headed to their designated areas.

Chapter Four:
The Escape Plan

Patty walked into the dark and dreary stairwell. Her skin was crawling with chill bumps as she ascended the stairs, heading upstairs to the second level. Reaching her designated landing, she had to use what little strength she had to open the door. Still not pulling hard enough, she used the crowbar that she had to help her pry open the door. She put her foot up on the wall and stuck the crowbar into the space between the door and the wall. After a few pulls, the door swung open and she flew back onto the floor.

"Ouch," she said as she laid on the floor in pain. After a few minutes of laying still, she managed to struggle to her feet. The good thing about it was that the trick worked. She turned her flashlight back on and walked through the door that was now halfway hanging off its hinges.

"This place is so icky," she said aloud. She saw a sign that informed her that she was on the floor which used to be the maternity floor.

She checked behind the desk and didn't see anything. So, she decided to go into the first room she saw. It still held a name card inside the clear box.

"McNair," she said aloud. "I wonder if this was Willie McNair's wife's room or something. Could be possible."

She continued into the room, allowing her flashlight to lead the way. She saw hospital blankets and sheets thrown all over the room. It was nothing like downstairs though. It wreaked of old vomit and filthy baby pampers. Patty couldn't put her hand on the other smell but whatever it was, it caused her to throw up in her mouth. She walked further into the room and decided to check the bathroom. The stench had grown stronger when she entered the area. Out of curiosity, she wanted to know what it was. She used her nose to guide her to the smell that was making her sick to her stomach. Surprisingly, it led her to the ceramic toilet. She hesitated for a second, not knowing what may be hiding inside. She silently counted to three then flipped the lid of the toilet. She shined her light inside. Right before her eyes, she saw feces, maggots, spiders, and roaches inside the commode. She screamed loudly and slammed the seat back down. She turned around and checked the shower. She pulled back the shower curtain and saw that there was no sign of Sammy in there either, just residue of hair left behind in the shower.

She exited the bathroom and went back into the room. She saw a patient chart lying on the air conditioning vent, and decided to take a peek at it. She looked at all the bloody fingerprints that aligned the folder and had second thoughts about it. Curious to know what information was inside burned a hole into her brain. She had an idea. She pulled the end of her sleeve over her fingers and used it to open up the folder. She read the first page from top to bottom.

"Samantha McNair. Age 30. Child's name: Christopher McNair, born October 29, 1973. Father's name: Willie McNair."

Wow, she thought. *This doesn't make any sense to me. Parker said that Marvin told him that a massacre happened here 45 years ago. How is that possible if this says that Willie McNair and his wife gave birth to a son?*

She continued reading the sheet out loud. "Christopher McNair's death date was later on that night." She flipped the paper over and underneath was a birth certificate for Christopher McNair, as well as

No Trespassing

a death certificate for both him and his mother, Samantha. "Oh my goodness. They both died, not just Christopher," Patty said aloud.

Before she could look more into the folder, she heard a low scream and footsteps running across the floor. Panicking, and practically jumping out of her skin, she dropped the patient chart and her flashlight. The flashlight hit the floor and she stood up against the air conditioning unit. Her breathing started to get heavy, and her heartbeat began to beat rapidly. She no longer heard the footsteps, but she could hear a voice. Like somebody was talking in a whisper so they couldn't be heard. She retrieved her flashlight from the floor and slowly tiptoed toward the door of the room.

"Melody, is that you?"

Melody did not respond.

"Parker? I know it's you. This isn't funny, you guys."

Parker wasn't there either.

She stopped in the middle of the room for a second and took a couple of deep breaths. "Marvin? Marvin, is that you? Are you guys trying to scare me? If you are, it's not working," she said with a quivering voice. Still, she heard nothing.

She stood at the entrance of the room and hesitated before peeking her head into the hallway. She poked her flashlight into the hallway and looked to the left, then to the right. Nobody was there. She left out the room and thought it would be a good idea to go into the next room. She walked slowly past the big window of the nursery. She thought she was seeing things out the corner of her eye, as a dark figure was on the opposite side of the glass. She didn't want to scream and draw attention to herself, so she held in her screams and replaced them with tears. She seen a door at the end of the hall.

That must be the emergency exit, she thought.

She steadied her breathing and not a second too early, she made a dash for the exit. She ran and ran and ran until she burst through the door and headed down the staircase. She wasn't sure if the person was following her or not, because she didn't hear any other footsteps but hers. She just wanted to get away and find one of her friends, and she wasn't gonna stop running until she did.

✶✶✶✶

"This is silly," Marvin said to himself as he walked through the basement of the hospital. "Who does Parker think he is, barking orders to people? He must have forgotten that I was his older brother. It's okay, though. I'm gonna get that little squirt back when he least expects it."

Marvin quieted down for a second as he made his way into a little room. He saw a fuse box on the wall. After the flick of a couple of switches, several lights turned on in the basement.

"That's better," he said smiling. He turned his flashlight off and pushed it down into his back pocket. He saw that he had reached a dead end, so he turned back around and headed back down the hall in the opposite direction.

"Morgue," he said reading a sign. "Oh, great. I got stuck where they stuff dead bodies. This should be fun." He pushed open the metal doors and saw big drawers that adorned the walls around the room. "Hey, Sammy, are you down here?" he asked in a hushed tone.

As low as he was talking, one would think he wasn't trying to disturb the dead. He walked over to the first wall of huge drawers. He opened them up one by one and they were all empty. He went to the other wall at the far right of the room. He opened the first drawer and thought that one would also be empty. But boy was he wrong. There was a body inside covered in a white sheet. He could see the tag hanging from the big toe that had the name "McNair" written on it. The toe looked as if was it was gonna fall completely off it was touched in any type of way. "That is disgusting," he said. He quickly covered his nose with his arm trying to block out the smell of the decayed body.

He looked over at the examination table and to his surprise, there was a box full of latex gloves. He ran over to the table and snatched two gloves out, placing them over his hands. He went back over to the drawer that held the body inside. Curious to find out if this was Willie McNair, it excited him. "If this is you, Willie, I am gonna be one rich guy. People have been looking for you for years. And to think you were here all of this time," he said, chuckling. He pulled the drawer out further, until it couldn't go any longer. He snatched the sheet from the corpse and saw that it was a woman. "Well, this sucks," he said with disappointment. "Then again, maybe this will still be worth a nice coin. But how will I have proof?"

He looked around the room until his eyes fell upon a wall that had different surgical tools aligning it. He walked over and thought about which of these scary instruments would do the job. He chose to go with one of the amputation knives. He grabbed it down from the wall, and admired the serrated edge of the blade. He smiled as he headed back over to the corpse.

He braced himself for the smell again. He had a quick flashback to a horror movie that he had seen before, and hoped that he could cut this head off as easily as the killer had done in the movie. He placed the amputation knife across the neck of the corpse, as he held his other arm up to his nose. He shut his eyes and squeezed them tightly

No Trespassing

together as he prepared to chop the head off. He lifted it a little and brought it down. He stopped midway when he heard something scuffling behind him. He froze in place and opened his eyes back up. He looked around, but there was no soul in sight.

He was about to try again for a second time when he heard the scuffling noise again. It was coming from the other side of the room. He kept the knife in his hand as he walked over to where the noise was coming from. He ended up at a coat closet. He slowly reached for the door handle. He snatched it open and saw rats running in and out of holes of a dead man's body. "Holy crap," Marvin yelled slamming the door back. He hastily walked back over to the dead body. Without hesitation, he chopped the head off with one try. He grabbed a small body bag, that was just big enough for the head and threw it inside. "Time to go," he said.

As he dropped the knife onto the floor and removed the gloves, he picked up the pole that he had came inside with. With the pole and the bagged head in his possession, he headed to the door. As he reached for the handle, he saw a shadow on the other side of the door. He couldn't make out who it was because the window was not able to be seen through. Whoever it was, they couldn't see him either. He waited a couple of seconds. He gathered up strength and courage before he gently opened the door and walked into the hall. A tall, hooded figure was only a few feet away from him and they never looked back. From the looks of the back of the person, Marvin knew that it couldn't have been neither his brother or Sammy, but from the walk, he knew it was definitely a man.

He slid the bag onto his wrist and got a tight grip on the pole with both hands. He walked quickly up to the person, unnoticed, and hit him. He aimed for the back of his legs first. The man fell to the ground and groaned. Marvin used this opportunity to pummel the man to a pulp. He hit him across the back several times. He didn't have time to see who it was, nor did he want the person to risk the person retaliating on him, so he high-tailed it down the basement corridor. He took one last look at the man laying on his stomach in the middle of the hall, motionless, before running up the stairs in search of Parker.

✳✳✳✳

Melody looked around on the main level, and was getting creeped out more than ever. She nearly jumped out of her skin when the lights had come on a little while ago. It was a little less creepy when they were all together, but now she felt as if she was casted in a horror movie. She was now entering the fourth room on this floor and it just so happened to be the office of the head doctor. She saw papers thrown all over the place.

"This place is a mess," she replied as she walked in a little more. She stepped on several patient charts and walked around a couple of flipped over chairs as she made her way over to the desk. She searched through drawers, looking for nothing in particular, just being plain old nosey Melody, as always. She pulled out an old book that looked to be a journal of some sort. She opened it to the entry for today's date, 45 years ago. There was so much dust covering the page that she had to blow on it. The dust flew into her eyes and she dropped the book onto the desk. As she rubbed her eyes to clear them, she heard a squeaking noise.

Were those sneakers? she thought. "Parker is that you? Patty? Marvin?" No one replied. A little frightened, she didn't let it get to her. She just picked the journal back up and began reading aloud.

"Dear Journal," it began. "This has been a rough day thus far. We have lost not only one life today, but two. It was extremely heartbreaking. It was the deaths of

a young mother and her newborn. She had informed the staff of nurses, and myself as well, that this was her first child. She wasn't nervous or anything, even though she was in active labor. She was as calm as the sea. She told us that she and her husband had been married for eight years and they had been trying to have children since then. After several miscarriages, they had finally been blessed with a baby boy. She named him Christopher McNair, after her husband's late father. He wasn't here yet. I think she said that his plane hadn't landed, or something of that nature. She had asked me to leave the baby in the room with her instead of the nursery so he would be there when her husband arrived. I told her we couldn't, but she wouldn't take no for an answer. I'm not sure what had transpired between the birth and now, but we just had to place white sheets over both the mother and her child. I had run tests on them both, only to find out that the mother had suffered from an infection and the child had an extremely high dosage of sodium chloride in its bloodstream. It was so hard to explain this once the father had finally arrived. It was a little awkward, though. He didn't yell, nor did he even shed a tear. He placed a kiss on each of the bodies and left the hospital without uttering a word."

She wanted to continue, but she couldn't. The couple of words that were beginning a new sentence, was covered in dark blood. She ran her fingers over the spots. It was hard and the page was crinkly beneath it. As she held the journal between her fingers, a tear escaped from her eye. It trickled down her face before landing on top of the blood that stained the page.

"That was so sad," she said to aloud to herself. "Maybe this is why that guy went ballistic on everybody. I would have, too." She wiped her face and put the book back into the drawer. She remembered that she had to help find Sammy. At least she knew now why that massacre had happened.

She got up from the desk and looked around the office some more. There still were no signs of Sammy, so she left out and headed back out to the lobby area. "There's one more room on this floor," she said. "Sammy you better come up soon. It's almost sunrise." She headed into the last room, hoping to find her friend once and for all. This room was nothing but the hospital pharmacy. There looked to be hundreds, maybe thousands, of various medications surrounding her as she walked into the room. She noticed the labels with the names on it and recognized some of them. The medicines ranged from Tylenol to Motrin to medicine for blood pressure. Melody looked at the clipboard hanging on the wall. She picked it up and saw all the signatures from the various doctors that worked here that picked up meds for their patients. Not one of these were signed off for anybody with the last name McNair.

"That's a little odd," she said, then placed the clipboard back onto the wall. There wasn't really anywhere for Sammy to hide in here; here was nothing but open space inside the room. It was time to give up.

She was walking quickly to leave the pharmacy, but halted as she heard footsteps running down the hall. She looked around nervously for a place to hide. There was no place to hide except under the table where they distributed medication to the doctors. She quickly dove under as the footsteps closed in on her. She put her hand over her mouth, covering it so whoever it was would not hear her hard breathing. She wished at this moment that she had had the bat that Parker had given her. She would have still been scared but she wouldn't have been this scared. Plus, she would have been able to protect herself. All she could see was feet enter the room and stop right in front of her. Her fear caused her to let out a warm stream of pee. It seeped through her clothes and made her cry. *I just ruined a three hundred dollar skirt,* she screamed in her head.

"Is anybody in here?" she heard a female voice say.

"Patty? Is that you, Pat?" she asked, peeping over the counter.

No Trespassing

"Oh my goodness, Mel," Patty said, running around to hug her friend. "*Ewww,* did you pee on yourself?"

Melody's face turned bright red as she responded, "Yes. I was scared and I thought you were Willie McNair."

"Well, I'm not. But he is here."

"What do you mean he's here? How do you know?"

"Well I don't know for sure. When I was upstairs I thought I saw somebody in the nursery. When I confirmed that I did, I just ran as fast as I could. Then I ran into you just now."

"I'm so glad you're okay," Melody said, hugging her again.

"So am I. Have you seen Marvin or Parker?"

"Nope. How about you?"

"Me neither. You think they're okay, Mel?"

"I hope so. Let me call Parker's phone."

She pulled out her cell phone and went through the call log until she found Parker's number. The phone rang four times before going to voicemail. "He didn't pick up. What if Willie has him?" Melody cried hysterically.

"Calm down. Let's not jump to conclusions. Let's try Marvin's number."

"Um, why do you have his number?"

"Really, Mel? If you must know, his parents gave it to me one day I was looking for Parker and they were both together. Honestly, this

No Trespassing

isn't the time to even ask questions like that. It's after 4 a.m. and the demolition will probably be starting in the next two hours." She dialed Marvin's number and his phone rang. Instead of hearing the ringing on the other end of the phone, the girls heard it in the hall.

"He's out there," Melody said running toward the door.

"Wait, Melody," Patty said in a whisper as she pulled her back. "How do you know that's Marvin?"

"His phone was ringing out here, duh."

"What if it isn't him? What if he came across Willie and he took his phone?"

"I didn't think about that."

"I know. Let's call it again and see if he answers." This time, when she dialed the number, it was literally outside the door. She eased the phone away from her ear and pushed Melody back a little. She got a good grip on her crowbar and jumped through the doorway, swinging.

"*Aahhh*!" Marvin yelled as he blocked the blows. "Have you lost your marbles?" he snatched the crowbar from Patty's hands and threw it across the floor.

"Sorry, Marvin. We thought you were the killer trying to kill us."

"If I were, you would have killed me first. *Sheesh*. Besides, I left the killer in the basement."

"What? You saw him?" the two girls asked simultaneously.

"Yeah."

"Was it Willie McNair?" Melody asked.

"I'm not sure. I hit him a few times and then I ran."

"What's in the bag?" Patty asked.

"A head," he replied bluntly.

"Who's head?"

"A lady who's last name is McNair. I think it might have been Willie McNair's wife or something."

"It probably is," Melody said. "I found a journal that had an entry about her. Have you seen Parker, Marvin?"

"No. He's probably still upstairs."

"Maybe we should head up there, too," Patty said. "We don't have that much time left, and we haven't come across anything that could lead us to Sammy."

"Well, let's go," Marvin said, slinging the bag over his shoulder. Melody and Patty walked as close to Marvin as they could as they walked to the end of the hall and up the staircase to the top floor.

✳✳✳✳

"Sammy? Sammy? Are you up here, buddy?" Parker yelled as he made his way through the hall of the top floor. His voice bounced off the walls and echoed throughout. He was on the floor where they treated people that were in critical condition. He walked into one of the surgery rooms. There was a tray that had different tools lying on top of it. He picked each one up individually and admired them. Most of them had spiderwebs on them that he had to blow off.

"This room is amazing, despite what occured here," he said out loud. He put the tools back onto the tray and went back out the room to search for Sammy somewhere else.

He went into the next room that was yet another surgery room, but this one was set up differently. This one had a bed with stirrups still up in the air. There was a huge stain of blood, dark and moldy, in the center of the bed. *I wonder what happened here,* he thought. So many thoughts were racing through his mind as he got up closer on the bed. *I wonder what it feels like.* As he was reaching out to touch the bloody surface of the bed, he heard muffles and scuffles behind him. He quickly ran out the room, thinking it was Sammy, and that he was in danger. When he got into the hall, the entire floor was empty.

"That's odd," he said. "I know for sure I just heard something." He walked away from the room and went into the recovery room.

"Sammy, are you in here, bud?" he asked as he pushed open the doors. There were about twelve beds in this room, but there was something strange about the room that had caught his eye. He looked from left to right as he took in the atmosphere. Everything before his eyes was clean. There was no blood residue anywhere, nor were there any spiderwebs or rodents like there were throughout the rest of the hospital. The room didn't even have a bad odor. It smelled like pine sol with a hint of lemon or something, and everything looking spanking brand new. It felt as if he had walked into a completely different hospital. He walked up to one of the beds and ran his hand up and down the steel railings, leaving smudged fingerprints along the way.

"This is uncanny," he said in a whisper. It was even more well lit then the other rooms he had been in. All of the beds were even made up as if somebody was getting ready to sleep in them. He was about to walk over to another bed, but the vibrating of his cell phone startled him.

"He-Hello," he said, answering the phone.

"Parker? Where are you?" Marvin asked.

"I'm still upstairs. Where are you?"

"We're in the stairwell coming to you now."

"We? You found Sammy?"

"No. It's just me and the girls."

"Well, I'm in the recovery room. You guys are not gonna believe what I found."

"What di-. Find?" Marvin asked. His phone was starting to break up.

"Hello? Marvin? Hello? Are you there?" *Click*. The phone hung up from call failure. He tried dialling his brother's phone back, but it kept going straight to voicemail. He gave up and put the phone back into his pocket. He walked further into the room and looked out the window. He thought he had seen somebody for a second, but he brushed it off.

"My imagination is getting the best of me," he said.

He felt a cold chill brush over his body and turned around in fear. There was nobody behind him, so he let out a sigh of relief. He was about to try calling his brother again, but he heard low moans. They

No Trespassing

were coming from outside of the room. He walked fast out the room and listened again. "There it is again," he said to himself as he made his way to where the noise was coming from. He called out Sammy's name once again.

"Help! Help!" he heard someone yelling from the other end of the hall.

He jogged down the hall, to the last room on the right. Before he could make it to the door, somebody jumped out and blocked him from entering. Parker fell backwards onto the ground and stared back at the person before him. They were tall and not moving a muscle. They were dressed in all black, with a hood over their head. Even though there was dim lighting surrounding him, Parker still couldn't make out the person's face. All he could see was his eyes and long beard.

"Who are you?" he asked.

The person remained silent.

Fearing for his life, Parker used his elbows to crawl backwards, away from the mysterious stranger. At first, they stood there watching him, then they followed behind. The slow paces began to turn into a power-walk. Parker flipped over and jumped to his feet, taking off down the hall. He tried to open the door, but it wouldn't budge. He stood there with his back against the door, trying to think about what he could do. The dark person had gotten closer and he tried the door. As the person placed a hand on his shoulder, he let out a loud scream. He still tried to get out the door as the person was pulling on his arm. He remembered the screwdriver in his pocket. He took his hand off the door and removed it from his left pocket. Without a second thought, he put the screwdriver into the air and brought it down into the person's leg. He released Parker and fell to the floor in agonizing pain. Parker used this as an escape. Before he could run back down the hall, Marvin grabbed him.

"*Aahhh!*" Parker yelled at the top of his lungs.

"Chill, Parker. It's just me, Marvin," he said, turning his brother around.

"Where are Patty and Melody?" Parker asked when he turned around and noticed that his brother was alone.

Marvin turned around. "They were just behind me a second ago."

Parker looked behind his brother at the ground. The mysterious person was gone. "Where's the guy?"

"What guy, Parker?" Marvin asked looking behind him.

"There was just a guy right here. He grabbed me and I stabbed him in the leg with my screwdriver."

"Did he have on a hood?"

"Yeah. How did you know?"

"I saw him in the basement earlier."

"Something weird is going on here."

"You can say that again."

"Help me! Somebody please!" There were the screams again.

"Come on, Marvin," Parker said, grabbing Marvin by the arm and pulling him to the end of the hall. Marvin didn't even resist, he just followed orders. They made it to the last room and found that the door was hard to open. Together, they leaned against the door until it flew open, causing them to fall through and land on top of one another.

"You're crushing me, Marvin," Parker yelled out in pain.

"Sorry," he said, hopping off his little brother's back. He reached out a hand to his little brother to help him up.

They looked around the room and it was in complete shambles. All the hospital furniture and tools were flipped over everywhere. It looked as if a fight had broken out in there. This room was the biggest of them all, excluding the recovery room. It had at least four closets, and Parker knew that Sammy was probably hiding in one of them. He and Marvin opened the first two doors and nothing was there but dust and musty clothing. They tried the next door, and inside were oxygen machines and cords that hooked to them. They arrived at the last door and hesitated before opening it. Since it was his best friend, Parker decided to open it. Low and behold, Sammy was for sure inside.

"Sammy!" the two brothers said in unison. Sammy was lying inside with a bandage wrapped around his ankle and his arm in a sling.

"What happened, Sammy?" Parker asked as he and Marvin helped him up from the floor. They carried him over to a chair that hadn't been flipped over.

"When we all ran out of here the other night, I tripped over a broken step and fell down them. I was trying to scream for you guys but you had already sped away on your bikes. Somebody picked me up and brought me back inside. I was yelling at the top of my lungs, but nobody heard my cries for help."

"Well, I'm here now," Parker said.

81   *No Trespassing*

"So am I," Marvin said defensively.

"Where are Melody and Patty?" Sammy asked.

"Marvin lost them."

"I did no such thing," Marvin shot back.

"Then where are they, Marvin?" Parker asked.

"I don't know."

"I rest my case." Parker pulled out his phone to check the time. "Holy cow! We only have an hour and a half to get out of here before the demolition team gets here."

"We have to hurry and find the girls," Sammy said, standing to his feet. "Ouch," he yelped out in pain.

"You're not gonna be able to go anywhere with those injuries," Parker said, sitting him back down.

"Well, I'm definitely not staying here. I wanna get out of here."

"And you will. Hold on for a sec," Marvin said as he ran out of the room. He returned moments later, pushing an old wheelchair. "Here you go." They both worked together to place Sammy in the wheelchair properly.

"Let's go find Patty and Melody and get out of here once and for all," Sammy said, and off they went.

Chapter Five:
Happy Halloween

The morning sun's rays were shining through the broken windows and the boards that covered the others. Sammy, Parker, and Marvin had been going from floor to floor in search of Patty and Melody. The only thing that they kept managing to come across were rats and spiders.

"This is taking forever," Sammy said.

"What are you complaining for?" Marvin asked. "It's not like you're walking around. We're doing all the walking and pushing you around."

"It's not my fault."

"Well, it sure isn't ours. Whose fault is it that you don't know how to jump from some stairs? If my life is in danger, I'm gonna be the first to get away. It doesn't matter if I'm hurt or not."

"Knock it off, Marvin," Parker yelled, breaking up their little dispute. "If there is gonna be blame put on anybody, put it on me. If it wasn't for me, Sammy wouldn't be hurt, Patty and Melody wouldn't be lost, and we wouldn't be here trying to outrun a serial killer."

Parker continued to push Sammy in the wheelchair while Marvin led the way for them, holding the metal pole in his hand. As they reached the first door, Marvin went to turn the handle and the lights went out.

"What the fudge?" Parker said and leaned up against the wall.

"Pipe down, Parker," Marvin said. "It must have been the fuse box. Give me a sec and I will be right back."

"Where are you going?" Sammy asked in a hushed tone.

"I'm going down here to turn the lights back on. Just wait here."

"I have a bad feeling about this, Parker," Sammy said. Parker didn't answer. "Parker? Did you hear me?"

"*Shhh*," Parker replied. "I hear somebody down here."

"Yeah, your brother. Remember?"

"It's not him, Sammy."

"How do you know?"

"Because the footsteps are coming from the other direction."

That was the end of Sammy's questioning. He remained quiet, along with Parker. Parker remained as still as he could as he could feel someone getting closer to him. They stopped directly behind him. It was like they knew he was standing there, even in the darkness. They had mild breathing. They stood behind Parker, breathing on his neck and causing chills to run down his spine. He turned his head towards the person, but kept the rest of his body still. The lights came back on, lighting the hallway back up. Everybody in the corridor screamed at the top of their lungs.

"Melody? Patty? You guys are okay," Parker said hugging his friends.

"Sammy!" the two girls squealed.

No Trespassing

"I'm glad you two are okay," Melody said.

"So are we," Sammy responded.

"Wait," Patty said, looking around. "Where's Marvin?"

"I'm right here," he said coming back down the hall swinging the pole in his hand. "What happened to you guys? You were right behind me. At least that's what I thought."

"We were behind you," Patty said. "The lights went off in the stairwell and I could feel someone pulling on me. I had fainted and woke up in a room. I don't remember what happened nor how I ended up there."

"Well, I do. We were close behind you and like she said, somebody grabbed her. I was pulling on her to save her and somebody else came up behind me and pulled me away."

"Why didn't either of you scream for me then? That would have made logical sense, right?"

"Yeah, it would have if our mouths weren't covered. They had their hands over our mouths, muffling our screams. We ended up in a dark room with no windows. Patty was unconscious, so I had to figure a way out by myself."

"So, how did you get out?" Sammy asked.

"Can you let me finish? Dang," Melody replied before continuing with her story. "Anyway, back to what I was saying, I had to figure out a way for us to escape. I crawled on my knees and felt around the room as I traveled through the darkness. I managed to find the flashlight that had fallen out of my pocket and turned it on. The room was empty. It had no furniture or anything, but it was weird. It smelled like fresh paint."

"Paint?" Parker said.

"Yeah," she continued. "I searched the room using my flashlight, until my eyes fell on Patty. She was lying on her stomach in a corner. I ran over to her and tried to wake her up by shaking her. It didn't work, so I slapped her."

"Thanks again, by the way," Patty said, rubbing her face where Melody had left her handprint on her cheek.

"I said I was sorry already, Pat." The three boys snickered with laughter. When she glared at them, they silenced their giggles and wiped the smirks from their faces. "Once I got her up, we used our bodies to break the door down. After awhile, it actually worked. We crept out of the room, unnoticed, and made our way back to where we last saw you. Unfortunately for us, you weren't there, none of you were. So, Patty was like 'we should roam through each floor and holler all of their names.' At the time, I thought that would be a bad idea just in case the people that captured us were still lurking about. Long story short, we found you all and now we have to get out of here," she said, taking a deep breath afterward.

"You're right," Parker said, looking down at his phone. He saw that it was almost 6 a.m. and they had to jet before they got caught. "Our dad's company will probably be here any minute."

The group of five made their way to the stairwell. Once they reached the top of the staircase, they all hoisted Sammy's wheelchair midway in the air and began carefully travelling down the steps with him. They reached all the way down to the landing of the second level, and dropped the wheelchair onto the ground. Parker and Marvin stuck their heads through the doorway first, checking to make sure the coast was clear. Once they confirmed it was, Melody walked through, pushing the wheelchair as Patty walked behind her.

"It looks different in the daylight," Patty said.

"Not really. You can just see the dust particles better. That's all that is," Marvin replied. Patty sucked her teeth and rolled her eyes at his comment.

"Hey? This isn't the same way we came last time," Parker said, looking around.

"You're right," Sammy said. "The entrance doors are way downstairs at the other end."

"And we have to pass all those spooky rooms?" Melody cried.

"That's the only way to get out, genius," Marvin said, laughing.

"Oh, hush up, Marvin. I am getting tired of your wisecracks," Melody shouted.

"And I'm tired of your whining. Act your age, why don't ya."

"Why don't you?"

"Cut it out, Marvin," Parker yelled, stepping in between them. "You, too, Melody. Look, everybody, we have no choice but to go that way. Unless you all wanna stay here," he said, looking around at everyone. They all exchanged looks amongst each other. "Alrighty, then. Let's get out of here."

They all turned and walked down the hall of the second level. They passed rooms that had the doors closed shut, wondering if someone was on the other side watching them. They made it to the middle of the hallway when they heard a slight noise coming from behind them.

"Who dares trespass on my property?" a deep, raspy voice said.

Their heart rates began to beat faster, as they slowly turned on their heels. Standing twenty yards away from them was the hooded guy from last night. Their eyes grew, practically popping out of their heads. They still couldn't make out his face, because the hood was pulled down so far over his face. The only thing they could see was his long white and gray beard that hung down to his chest. His clothes were all dirty and tattered. He had no shoes on. The skin on his feet looked hard and stone-like. His toenails were under all of his toes and looked as though they were made of wood. The five kids stood there, motionless and frozen in their tracks, contemplating on what to do next. As soon as the figure took one step closer to them, they all ran away screaming. They ran into one of the hospital rooms and locked the door.

"Where's Sammy?" Parker yelled. Everybody looked around the room.

"He must still be out there," Patty said.

"You left him out there by himself?" Parker yelled as he stepped up to Melody.

"I panicked. I'm sorry," she said, crying frantically.

"This is unbelievable," Parker replied.

"Help! Parker? Melody? Marvin? Melody? Anybody! He's getting closer," Sammy screamed from the hall.

Parker paced the floor trying to come up with a plan. "Screw this," he said after a few moments. He snatched the pole from his brother's hand and pushed the girls from out front of the door.

"What do you think you're doing, Parker?' Marvin said, pulling his brother by the arm. Parker snatched his arm out of his grip.

"I'm going to save my best friend. That's what I'm doing."

"You're gonna mess around and get yourself killed," he said.

"At least I died trying," Parker replied before opening the door. He ran up behind Sammy's wheelchair just as the strange figure was approaching him. "Duck, Sammy," Parker yelled. Sammy ducked down in the chair as much as he could as Parker swung the pole. But he missed the guy. That didn't stop him though. He walked toward the man, as the man backed away, swinging the pole. The man ended up falling over an overturned chair and Parker went to work on the guy. He hit him multiple times in the legs, back and head with the metal pole.

"Stop, stop, stop," the man yelled. Parker still had the pole raised up in the air, waiting to see if he was gonna be attacked by the man. Parker turned him over onto his back.

"Holy crap," Parker said as he removed the hood from the mysterious stranger. "Guys come out here. And hurry!" he yelled to the others. Marvin, Melody, and Patty emerged from the room. Patty grabbed a hold of Sammy's wheelchair and pushed him down the hall to where Parker was.

"Oh, my goodness," Melody said as her hand flew up to her mouth.

"Is that Petey?" Patty asked walking closer to the guy on the floor.

"It is Petey."

"Who is Petey?" Marvin asked.

"He's some homeless guy that we feed after school and give spare change to."

"He's not just some homeless guy," Melody said. "He's our friend," she said sitting him up on the floor.

"So, wait a minute. You guys mean to tell me that you befriended a homeless guy? Are you all nuts?"

"No," Parker yelled. "Some people do have a heart, you know!"

"You should grow one, Marvin," Patty said.

"If he's your so-called friend, Parker, then why did he try to kill us?"

"I never tried to kill any of you," Petey said, coughing up blood. It came out of his mouth and landed in his beard and on the floor.

"But you were down in the basement," Marvin said to Petey.

"Yeah, I was. But you attacked me, kid."

"Oh, yeah. Sorry about that."

Petey struggled to get to his feet but he made it after a few attempts. "What are you all doing in here anyway?"

"We were here to find our friend, Sammy," Parker said pointing to Sammy.

"Yeah, and you kidnapped him," Patty said, stepping into Petey's face. When she saw the grim look on his face, she backed up and stood behind Marvin and Parker.

"Kidnapped? I didn't kidnap anybody. I was just merely trying to help the kid. Why would I hurt people that feed me five days a week?" he laughed a little. He smiled at the group, exposing his rotten gums and empty spaces where teeth once were.

"You guys hear that?" Parker said listening. Everyone stood still and quiet as they listened on. They felt the ground underneath of them vibrating, feeling like an earthquake was taking place. "That must be the demolition team. We have to get out of here." Petey and the kids started to panic.

"How are we all gonna get out of here in time? Look at Petey? And Sammy's in a wheelchair," Melody screamed over the loud noises outside.

"Maybe we can come back for Petey," Marvin said.

"We can't just leave him here. Are you crazy?" Parker yelled.

"How are we gonna get Sammy out of here?" Patty asked eye-balling the wheelchair.

"The same way we got him down here," Marvin said. "We carried him and the wheelchair down here."

"Uh-uh," Melody replied. "There is no way that I will be able to do that. My entire body is still in pain from bashing that door down upstairs."

"We're all gonna help," Parker intervened.

"Exactly, Melody," Marvin jumped in. "We're supposed to be working as a team to get out of here."

"I guess so," she said, crossing her arms like a child and stomping towards the wheelchair.

"What if your little friend tries to kill one of us again?" Marvin chimed in.

"He just said he wasn't trying to hurt anybody," Sammy said with a slight chuckle.

"Don't laugh at me, Sammy. This isn't a game," Marvin said angrily.

"Everybody just stay close together. We're gonna get out of here. Okay?"

"Okay," they all murmured.

Marvin and Parker pushed Sammy to the end of the hallway, while Patty and Melody hoisted Petey over their shoulders and carried him. Just as they hit the door where the stairwell was, the end of the hospital where they had just come from had crashed in. They were startled as they looked and saw the wrecking ball lying in the place of the wall.

"We have to hurry, everybody," Parker yelled over the bulldozers that had just turned on. The girls hurried down the stairs as fast and as carefully as they could with Petey. Marvin and Parker was right behind them with Sammy in the wheelchair.

"Crap," Marvin yelled.

"What happened?" Patty said, stopping and looking back. The wheelchair had slipped out of Marvin's grasp and Sammy was lying on the steps on his back.

"*Aahh*!" Sammy yelled out. "Parker help me," he said, reaching his hand out. Parker kicked the chair out of the way and he and Marvin threw Sammy over their shoulders like the girls had Petey. It was a little more difficult though, because of Sammy's banged arm.

They made it to the first level, where the main entrance was, just as they heard another crashing noise upstairs. They opened the door of the stairwell and watched as the ceiling was falling apart. It was shaking uncontrollably from all of the heavy machinery outside. They made it to the middle of the hall and Melody slipped and fell.

"My ankle," she said, screaming. "I think it's sprained," she cried.

"Oh, wow," Marvin said. "We have to get out of here, guys."

"We can't just leave her here," Patty yelled at him.

"And I don't wanna die either."

"You are so selfish," Patty said, pushing him.

"Hey, watch it," Sammy yelled.

"We don't have time for this," Parker interrupted. "Patty? You and my brother get Sammy out of here. I'll stay and help Melody."

"But what about Petey?" she asked, looking at the frail individual lying inches away from them on the floor.

"Just leave me here to die. Nobody cares about me," Petey said. "I have nothing to live for anymore."

"Don't talk like that, Petey," Parker said. "We're gonna get you out of here, too."

"Parker, I'm not leaving here without you. The ceiling is caving in too fast," Marvin said. "You may be a crybaby and a brat, but you're my little brother, and I love you."

"Good to know, Marvin. But right now, I have to do what I have to do. And what you need to do is get Sammy and Patty out of here. We'll be right behind you."

"See you outside, Parker," Marvin said. He and Patty lifted Sammy over their shoulders and carried him outside the building as the ceiling fell behind them.

"How are we gonna get out of here, now, Parker?" Melody asked. "The door is blocked."

"We're not gonna let that stop us. Can you walk at all, Mel?"

"Maybe, but not that fast, I'm sure," she replied. He helped her to her feet. "I'm gonna help you with Petey."

"No. You go ahead behind the others."

"But what about you?"

"I'll be fine. You just get out of here," he said, raising his voice a little.

"Okay. Hurry up and get out here," she said.

"We're gonna be right behind you." He watched Melody as she limped to where the ceiling had fallen in at. She climbed over the mountain of rubble as she made her way outside.

"Melody? You're here, too?" Parker's father yelled at her. She looked and saw her friends standing next to Marvin at an ambulance. It looked like they had already gotten chewed out before and after they got their wounds treated.

"Yes. Sorry, Sir."

"Your parents will be hearing about this. But never mind that, where in the world is Parker?"

"He's still inside."

"What? Hold the wrecking ball," he yelled at one of his employees.

"What's the matter, Boss?" his head foreman James asked as he walked up to him.

"My son is in there!" he said, grabbing him by the shirt.

"How do we proceed, Sir?"

"You don't! Let me get my son out of there first," Eliot removed his construction hat and ran inside the building after his son. "Parker? Parker?" he yelled out as he climbed down the pile of rubbish.

"Dad? I'm over here," he said, standing in the middle of the floor with Petey leaning onto his small frame.

"What happened, Parker?"

"Dad, right now, there is no time to explain. That last hit this building received is causing it to fall quickly. I need your help getting him out of here."

"Who is he?" Eliot asked throwing Petey's other arm over his neck.

"I said I will explain everything later. Just know that none of this is Marvin's fault."

"I highly doubt that, Parker. You're all in big trouble."

"We know. We can discuss my punishment later."

"You bet we are."

Parker and Eliot made their way to the exit. Eliot had to climb to the top of the pile of rubble and pull Petey up by his arms. Once Petey was on the other side, Eliot reached down for Parker. Before he could grasp Parker's hand, the ceiling fell down on him.

"Parker!" he yelled. He quickly jumped down and threw pieces of the ceiling across the room, trying to dig Parker out.

"I'm right here, Dad," he said in a low voice. His father pulled him from the floor and threw him over his shoulder. He slipped a couple of times climbing out but he finally made it onto the other side.

"Parker!" Melody squealed. They all went over to him as his father sat him on top of one of the gurneys. "I'm so glad you're okay," she said, throwing her arms around his neck.

"I'm glad you're okay, too, Parker," Patty said, hugging him as well.

"You saved us, Park. That was pretty awesome," Sammy said, giving his best friend a high five.

"Yeah, you did it, little bro," Marvin agreed. "I'm proud of you, Parker. I can't call you a whiny little wimp anymore, I see."

"Nope, you can't. I proved to all of you that I wasn't a chicken and that I could be brave."

"Yeah you did," Sammy said.

"Next time you wanna prove how brave you are, go ride a roller coaster or something. *Sheesh*," Melody said. The group of friends broke out into laughter.

"I'll make sure to do that," he replied. After the paramedic finished bandaging him up, their father came over. He looked at them all with a stern look.

"Explain," he said, folding his arms across his chest.

"Well, it's like this, Dad, I asked everybody to come with me and stay an entire night with me. The first time we came, we got scared and ran out but Sammy got left behind. So, we had to come back and get him and get out of here before you got here so we wouldn't get caught."

"But you still got caught. And why did you come here in the first place? I don't think you disclosed that to me yet."

"Well, I was just tired of everybody calling me a chicken and a big baby. So, I chose to stay the night at Grady to prove them wrong."

"Parker, that's the craziest nonsense I have ever heard in all my days. You could have been hurt, or worse. What were you thinking?" he asked. He continued to talk before even giving Parker a chance to respond. "You weren't thinking, were you? No. Because, if you were using your brain, none of you will be in this predicament in the first place. And who is that guy over there, anyway?" he asked, pointing in the direction of Petey.

"Oh, that's just Petey. He's a friend of ours."

"He's a homeless man, Parker. What did your mother tell you about talking to strangers? And what about all of your parents?" he asked Sammy, Melody, and Patty. None of them responded to his question. They just hung their heads low and diverted their eyes to the ground in shame.

"I'm sorry, Dad. It will never happen again."

"I know it won't ever happen again. You're grounded until the end of time," he yelled. "And so are you, Marvin."

"Me? Why am I grounded? I didn't do anything. I came to make sure my little brother was okay," Marvin said, trying to defend himself.

"It doesn't matter, Marvin. I don't wanna hear it. You should have come to me or your mother when you found out they were coming here."

"They had already come here before I found out, Dad. He came to me saying that they lost Sammy."

"And did you come to us then?"

"No, Sir."

"Then I rest my case." He looked at Sammy and the girls. "And I hope you three learned your lessons as well. You all are too smart to be doing something so dangerous. I hope next time you all think before you do something this drastic again."

"We will. And we're sorry, Mr. Wilson," Patty said.

"So am I," Melody said.

"Yeah, me, too, Mr. Wilson," Sammy said.

No Trespassing

"Anyway, we have to get back to work. You all call your parents and tell them where you are so they can come and get you. Sammy and Melody, I hope you two get better soon." He stepped in front of Parker and Marvin. "And as for you two, I'm sure your mother would love to hear about your adventurous weekend. And don't leave out any details."

"Yes, Sir," the two brothers said in unison. He walked away and got back to his demolition crew.

"I should pound your face in," Marvin said, grabbing Parker by the shirt.

"Hey, nobody told you to come, Marvin. By the way, where's your head?"

"Oh, crap," he said. "I left it in there. I need to go in there and get it," he said limping away. Parker and his friends just laughed at him as he went up to Mr. Wilson and begged him to go inside and get the head.

Parker walked away from his friends for a second and went over to the ambulance where Petey was. "How are you feeling, Petey?" he asked.

"Oh, I'm okay, I guess. I'm living," he said, laughing through coughs.

"Yeah," Parker said, laughing along with him uneasily. "I'm really sorry I hit you with the pole. Oh, and for stabbing you."

"It's okay, kid. I know you were just doing what you had to do to protect you and your friends."

"No hard feelings?" Parker asked, reaching his hand out to him.

No Trespassing

"No hard feelings at all," Petey said, shaking his hand. "I'll see you around."

"You will see me on Monday after school. Same time? Same place?"

"I'll be there," Petey said. He watched as Parker went over and joined his brother and his friends. "They are such sweet kids," he said aloud. "I just wish they weren't so nice to me."

"Excuse me, Sir? You're gonna need to go to the hospital for examination."

"I can't go there," Petey replied.

"Are you refusing medical attention, Sir?"

"Refusing? I can't afford it."

"You are an elderly person, I'm pretty sure the state insurance will cover you and any medical bills that you may receive."

"I hear you," Petey said, climbing down off the gurney.

"Where are you going, Sir?"

"I told you, I cannot afford the hospital. Heck, I can't even afford to sit up on your fancy paramedic bed. I'll be just fine," he said. He took three steps and doubled over in pain. The female paramedic ran over to him and helped him back to the ambulance.

"Look, Sir, I don't care what you say. You are going to the hospital and you are going now," she said. With the help of another paramedic, she was able to strap him on the gurney and put him in the back of the ambulance. She quickly hooked up an oxygen mask to his face for precaution. As the ambulance rode away from the ashes that were once Grady Hospital, Petey noticed that Parker's mother and the other parents had arrived. His eyes zeroed in and locked in on Elaine. She looked all too familiar. As he dug into his thoughts he remembered who she was.

How on earth could I ever forget such a beautiful creation of God? he thought to himself. He remembered the last time he had seen her. He was walking past her when Grady Hospital was still open. She was the only nurse with brunette hair. She had freckles on both cheeks and brown eyes that matched her hair perfectly. Her skin was fair and her face reminded him of a cherub. He also remembered that the last time they locked eyes, she had tears in hers. She had shed enough tears for the both of them, as she apologized thousands of times for his losses.

After 45 long years, Petey finally shed a tear for the loss of his family. He had not only lost his wife, but his first and only child as well. And it was all his fault that he had missed out seeing them for one last time. He treated his company as a top priority rather than his wife and child. He walked around with regret all of these years. He laid back on the gurney and closed his eyes.

I'm sorry, he said to himself as his apology went up to the heavens to his wife and son. He felt relieved to finally be able to do that after all this time. The ambulance went over several speed bumps and turned so many corners before they arrived at Lincoln Memorial Hospital in Lakewood. That was over thirty minutes from where he slept every day.

"Okay, Sir, we're here," the female paramedic said. "We just have to wait a few moments so they can get you a bed ready. Is that okay with you?"

"Sure, it's fine. I'm just happy to have somewhere warm to sleep tonight."

"Okay so can you tell me your name, Sir?"

"It's Willie. Willie McNair."

The paramedic froze in the middle of writing down his name on the paperwork. She looked at him and he stared back at her with the most evil grin she had ever seen in her life.

ABOUT THE AUTHOR

American author Rachelle Jarred is entranced by the magic of written words. She's had an unflinching love for writing since she was seven, and now lives her dream of being a published author and a poet. Writing is more than just her career; it's her way of life.

Rachelle prides herself on exploring multiple fiction genres. With sizzling hot erotica, blood-cuddling horror, and scintillating suspense, she has enticing packages for every book lover. She is looking forward to diving into children's stories in the near future.

She was born and raised in Washington, D.C., and currently works full-time as the CEO of BluGem Publishing where her books are published. Between her writing career and her life as a mother of two, Rachelle enjoys spending time with her loved ones and always makes time to help new authors find their way in the writing industry. She currently resides in Prince George's County, Maryland.

www.ingramcontent.com/pod-product-compliance
Lightning Source LLC
Chambersburg PA
CBHW052141220626
47052CB00005B/1142